A CAPFUL O' NAILS

DAVID CHRISTIE MURRAY

A BLACK COUNTRY SOCIETY PUBLICATION

First impression 1973

Second impression 1977

ISBN 0 904015 00 9

Cover design by Roger Manning

Printed by Reliance Printing Works, Halesowen, West Midlands

THE AUTHOR

David Christie Murray was born in High Street, West Bromwich in 1847 and commenced his career as a journalist on the Wednesbury Advertiser — for free! He worked his way up to become a war correspondent and in 1877 reported on the Russo-Turkish war for the *Chicago Times.*

His first novel appeared in 1879 and 'A Capful O' Nails' was published in 1896.

He died in London in 1907 and failed to win the acclaim of his native town beyond a memorial tablet in West Bromwich Central Library. Belatedly, this re-print by the Black Country Society helps to redress the balance.

PREFACE

THIS little book was written in dead earnest, and on re-reading it, a year or two after its completion, I am forced to own that it might have been more attractive as a work of art if its singleness of purpose had been less apparent. But the work is done, and it is too late now to meddle with it. The blot on English life with which it deals is lighter by many shades than it used to be, but it is still dark enough in all conscience. In its main lines the tale is quite true; and in my childhood, many of its people were familiar to me. I have written of what I knew, and I have nowhere exaggerated by one hair's breadth. Much is amended nowadays, but the truth, even to-day, is stern and mournful, and may well make an Englishman ashamed.

DAVID CHRISTIE MURRAY.

London, Sept. 1896.

CHAPTER I

A BETTER man than my father never lived. After many years, I have the chance to do his memory justice. I do not suppose that any very great number of people will interest themselves in a career so lowly as his was, but here and there one of those who knew him may understand him from these pages, and here and there a stranger may learn to sympathize with as true, as brave, and as gentle an English heart as ever beat.

He was a nailmaker, and we lived in a field opposite the brick-kilns on the road between Castle Barfield and Quarrymoor. It goes without saying that we were miserably poor, for in his day there was no class of workman so vilely paid as that to which he belonged. Even in this age of progress the condition of the nailmaker is not very much mended; but I know that my father and mother, though they worked literally day and night, never earned as much as thirteen shillings in a single week between them. There was one red letter week, often talked about when I was a child, in which their joint earnings had mounted to twelve and ninepence.

We were in the middle of a row of cottages, and there was no hour of the twenty-four in which you could not hear the clink of the little hammer on the anvil. Each cottage had two rooms; the front-room opening on the street was dining-room, sitting-room, and bedroom in one. The room at the back was the work-shop. It was fitted with a small forge and bellows and four or five very small anvils. Ours was the only cottage in the row in which all the members of the family did not work together. The children of our neighbours began almost in infancy. I have seen a girl of seven turning out her tale of wrought nails six days out of every seven that God sent, and the boys were taught to use a hammer as soon as they could understand anything.

We lived opposite the brick-kilns, and the air was always heavy with smoke and the sickening smell of burning clay. I do not know if the baking of bricks everywhere creates such a stench as it did there. Perhaps there was some peculiar quality in the clay of that district, but the odour was frightful, and wayfarers passing the brick-kilns would run for a hundred yards, pinching their noses with thumb and forefinger. I have known strangers to be absolutely sickened in passing, but we who lived there were accustomed to the abominable air, and paid no heed to it, though I think that it had something to do with our general ill-health and stunted growth.

When I was very young indeed, I remember thinking that our little neighbourhood was like a sore place on a body otherwise healthy, for the country round about us was as pretty and smiling as any to be found in mid-England. We had more time to explore it than the children of our neighbours, for father never let one of us lay hand on hammer. He sent us all to school at Quarrymoor, though the threepence per week we cost him must have been an awful drain on his poor resources. Heaven only knows what a constant long-drawn and heroic pain it must have been to him and mother to find the weekly ninepence that was spent in schooling. It was found somehow, and from my fifth birthday to my twelfth I can only remember one week when I had to stay away from school for want of the stipend.

The forge in the back-kitchen was my earliest memory. I awoke permanently to a knowledge of the world whilst mother was working at the anvil. I was fixed in a sort of cloth bag upon her shoulders, and I remember peering round her neck at the glow of the fire, watching the iron rod as it came white-hot from the white-hot coke, and seeing her shape the end with dexterous blows into a nail, and then plunge the rod back into the fire again. It was raining at the time, and the splash on the roof made a dismal and sullen sound. I was hungry and I cried; but I was deeply interested for all that. Father came in wet and bare-headed, carrying in his hands a ragged cap full of coke, which he had bought or borrowed from a neighbour. I can see the place as I write. I can hear the tinkle of the hammer and its multiplied echoes from the cottages of our neighbours. The very odour of the place is back in my nostrils, and I could almost cry to think of the sordid squalor in which the lives of the two bravest and gentlest creatures I have ever known were spent.

I was not very old when I learned that father was a marked man in two ways. He enjoyed an extraordinary esteem amongst his neighbours, and I heard wonderful stories about his scholarship. He could read and write and cast accounts, and he had a rare gift of speech, which I dare say came to him by nature, though it was no doubt improved by his studious habits. A full half of a nailer's time is taken up by the purely mechanical work of the bellows, and father always had a book propped up against the wall in such a position that he could read a line or two of it whilst so engaged. He was a swift and dexterous workman, and this form of study never seemed to impede his labour. Whilst he shaped the nail, he would repeat to himself in an undertone the line or two he had just read, and would take up the context when he turned round to the bellows and the fire. I had, of course, in my earlier days, no knowledge of the books he studied, but I found out later that he was deep in Adam Smith and Ricardo, and that Mill's 'Liberty', then a new book, was a prime favourite with him. All day and every day, Sundays excepted, he read and hammered, and from dawn till dark on Sundays he sat with the book before him. If our neighbours had an ignorant admiration for his learning, his main employer, Mr. Sim, had a more than equally, ignorant contempt for it. I got to know Mr. Sim on my seventh birthday, and I shall never forget my introduction to him whilst I remember anything.

I was born on the first day of June, and my seventh birthday opened in perfect weather. The trees and hedges on the road to Quarrymoor were in their freshest and tenderest green. The sun was shining and the birds sang, and the hedgerows were thick with wildflowers and fern. There was a wonderful pink hawthorn, generations old, and father broke off a branch of it for me. He carried a capful of nails in his hand, and was on his way to sell them. Things had been pretty bad with us for a week or two, for both he and mother had been out of sorts, and we had been living in a more than usual hand-to-mouth fashion.

'Jack,' said he to me, 'what's three times seven?'

I answered, ' Twenty-one.'

' You're a third part of a man to-day, Jack,' he said, taking my soft chin between his horny thumb and forefinger, and turning my face towards him. ' This day fourteen 'ears you'll have come to man's estaät. I'm not goin' to frighten thee, Jack, but how's schoolin' gettin' on? '

I felt stupid, and said nothing, but in my inmost heart I thought that schooling was getting on very well indeed. The boys with whom I had opportunity of comparing myself knew so little that I, who could read the newspaper without stumbling, felt like a monster of erudition.

' Theer's nothin' like learnin', Jack,' said my father. ' If I'd had the luck to learn to read an' write when I was thy age, I should niver ha' been where I am now. I had to pick it up piecemeal after I was thirty. Open your mind lad. Read an' think, an' niver tek things for gospel acause ye see 'em in a book. Fight out iverything in your own mind, my lad, an' niver be afraid o' your own thoughts. There was a great lord once as said, " Readin' makes a full man, thinking a wise un." It's no use readin' onless ye think o' what ye read.'

He said much more, of which I understood little at the time, but which went to the general effect that a man's mind was the only kingdom a man could really govern and enjoy.

We had a walk of a mile and a half to make before we came to Mr. Sim's house in Quarrymoor. It stood in the middle of the straggling hilly High Street, and, being two stories high and built of the local stone, had a palatial look to my eyes. We entered by the back way through a gate which led to an ill-conditioned garden. The kitchen door was open, and there was a scent upon the air which I had never before encountered. I was normally hungry, but this odour made me ravenous, though I had not a guess at the moment as to what created it. I know now that it meant hot duckling with a stuffing of sage and onions. The duckling, or a part of it, lay yet on the dish, and Mr. Sim sat behind it, knife and fork in hand. He was a man whose complexion was made up of oil and grime, and as he shovelled green peas into his mouth with the blade of his knife, a little rivulet of gravy trickled down his bristly chin. He was very corpulent, and had a over-fed look which I remember to have thought offensive. He said ' Hillo! ' as we entered the kitchen, and stared at us both with hard, uninterested eyes whilst he shovelled at the green peas.

'I've got five hundred two-inch number fives,' said father, opening the cap he carried and holding it in both hands.

'All right,' said Mr. Sim, with his mouth full. 'Wait i' the yard till I can find time to come t' ye'.

Father obeyed, and sat on the stone trough of the pump for perhaps ten minutes. At the end of that time or thereabouts, Mr. Sim came out with a key in his hand. He unlocked the door of an outhouse which stood in one corner of the garden. This place was well stocked with bundles of rod-iron of various thicknesses, such as nailers use, and in the middle of the room was a rough counter with a pair of scales on it. Mr. Sim emptied the nails from the cap into the scale, and weighed them with a great air of scrupulousness.

'Five pound fourteen hounce,' he said at last.

'Siven pound,' said father, very quietly.

Mr. Sim let fall a weight he had in his hand, and stared as if wonderstricken. Father met his look with a quiet steadiness, and my heart began to quake, for I saw already that there was a quarrel. Mr. Sim was a great man in my eyes at this time, for I could not remember an hour when our leave to live did not appear to depend upon his favour. He was almost father's only customer.

'Siven pound,' said father, after a pause.

Mr. Sim thrust his hand into his pocket and began to count out money from an overflowing fistful of silver and copper.

'Five pound fourteen hounce,' he said. 'Tek it or leave it.'

'I've had them nails weighed twice to-day,' father answered. 'They turned the scale at seven pound.'

'Well, I'm damned!' said Mr. Sim, looking round with a dull exasperation in his face. 'This is apretty state o' things. Beggars has come to be choosers, eh? Now, don't yo' give me no more o' your lip, Salter. Five pound fourteen hounce. Tek it or leave it.'

'Wait a bit,' said my father. He took up the weight Mr. Sim had allowed to fall on the rough counter, and balanced it in his hand. 'That's four pound, is it?' he asked. 'And this,' seizing another weight at the end of the counter as he spoke, 'is another four pound. We'll see how they tally, Mr. Sim!' He was in the act of gathering up the nails from the scale, when Mr. Sim came round the counter and shouldered him on one side.

'Keep your hands off my property, Salter.'

'Theer's a good pound difference between 'em,' said my father, with a sudden flash of anger. 'When I buy rods it's three an' a half pound weight for four. When I sell nails it's four for three an' a half.'

Young as I was, I was so familiar with this fact, and had always understood so clearly that this was regarded as a custom of the trade, that I really thought father a little unreasonable in being angry at it. People grumbled about it sometimes, as they did about wet weather or cold, or the price of coke and bread, which were the two essentials of life to us. But I had never been taught to regard any of these things as being changeable by any effort of ours.

'I've seen you on the down'ard road a long time, Salter,' said Mr. Sim. You're marked out a'ready for a sort of Radical hatheist, and you'll soon find out wheer you're goin' to. You ought to know by this time which side your bread's buttered on.'

'Buttered!' said my father, with a short and angry laugh. 'Bittered'd be more like it. Theer's no butter for the likes o' thee and me, Jack.'

'Git out o' my ware'us,' said Mr. Sim, 'an tek your rubbidge with ye. Theer's no wuss nailer for five miles round. A workman,' continued Mr. Sim, addressing himself to the doorway and the open air 'as I've kept goin' out o' charity for 'ears and 'ears.'

Father made no reply to this, but gathering up the nails, returned them to the cap, and, pushing me gently before him, walked into the garden. Mr. Sim slammed and locked the door, and followed angrily.

'Don't yo' come anigh me no more,' he shouted. 'I niver want to see thy ugly mug again, Jack Salter.'

There were half a dozen loungers in the street, and at the sound of the fogger's voice raised in anger they drew near. The fogger, I should tell you, is a petty dealer in the trade, and I have always thought the word an abbreviation of pettifogger. It may have a quite different derivation, but if so I am at fault.

'It's took me some years,' said father, 'to mek up my mind. I've stood your wicked tyranny, like hundreds more o' the poor souls about here, for the sake o' the wife and children. I'll stand it no more. There isn't a man in your trade, Mr. Sim, as isn't a daylight robber.'

'I'll mek you prove them slanderin' words!' cried Mr. Sim, advancing wrathfully.

'I shall ask nothin' better,' said father, 'than to have the chance of proving 'em. I should ask nothin' better than the chance of mekin' all English ears to tingle with your villainies.'

'Why, Salter, Salter!' said a quick authorative voice, 'what's this?'

The voice spoke right over my head, and looking up, I saw a gaunt man in black. We had little chance of seeing gentlemen in our part of the world, but ignorant and unpractised as we were, none of us had any difficulty in recognising a gentleman in Mr. Allardyce. He was the curate of the parish church, and there was a vague popular mistrust in him, because he was supposed to be more than half a 'Papish.' Father had a profound respect for him, and that was more than enough for me. I doubt if any other man of his class in our district could have given the feeblest idea of what a 'Papish' was, and how he differed from people who were not 'Papishes.'

Mr. Allardyce spent his life, and more than half his narrow stipend, amongst the poor; but he was High Church, and the *odium theologicum* stood between him and his people. He was quite fresh from Oxford, and as I learnt long afterwards, had been under the personal influence of a band of saintly and earnest men who were at that time execrated throughout the length and breadth of the Empire. It was curious that the history of a gentleman and a scholar should have been bound up with that of a man in my father's position but Mr. Allardyce found his fate that day. It led him through dreadful tribulation, but I do not believe he ever knew a moment's regret for the action he took.

'Why, Salter, Salter! whats' this?' said Mr. Allardyce.

In the High Street of Quarrymoor you were everywhere within reach of the wheezing noise of the little bellows which blew the fires of coke and slack; and you could always hear, at any hour of the day and night, the tinkle of the little hammer on the little anvil. But by this time, the sounds of labour within hearing were suspended, and men and women, girls and boys and little children, came to the doors and looked out into the street. They were all unkempt and grimed, and mostly stunted. Some of the iron-workers were younger than myself. I have always looked back on that time with a profound sense of pity, and I remember one labour-stained girl, who could be no more than five years of age, standing shading her eyes against the sunlight, with a little hammer in her hand.

'I tell ye what it is, sir,' said my father. 'I've browt my mind to it at last; I shan't care what it costs me—I've got my word to speak an' I shall speak it.'

There was an empty wheelbarrow standing in the roadway beside him. He stepped into it, and raised his voice:

'Mr. Allardyce, and friends and neighbours,—It's full time somebody spoke a word. Mark ye this: the man as speaks the word is ruined. I know what's in front o' me—I'm a marked man from this minute. I see what lies afore me. It may be starvation, it may be the workus. Be it what it may, here's my word.'

The street was full by this time. There was a crowd of at least a hundred, and people were running towards us from both sides.

'I say naught,' pursued my father, 'agen any man in particular, but from this minute out I'm goin' to fight agen a wicked system. What are we, friends, but dumb cattle? '

The audience gaped and stared with grimy, unintelligent, uninterested faces.

'Mr. Allardyce,' my father continued, 'I've told you in private, many and many's the time, the whull history o' this business. Now I'll tell ye in front o' them that knows. Here's the fogger's game wi' the Black-Country nailer. To begin with, he's got three sets o' weights: a light set to buy with, a heavy set to sell with, and another set to show th' inspector when he comes his rounds. He's forbid by law to keep a tommy shop, but there ain't a fogger in the countryside as hasn't got a relation in that line o' business. We're forced to buy bad and dear, or woe betide us. When we buy for a certain size o' nail, they sell us rods too thick for use, and charge us for changing them. They give us light weight, to begin with, and they lighten light weight till you've got sixpenn'orth for ninepence. When it comes to sellin' thc nails, they use the heavy weight, and they tek twelve hundred for a thousand. They're not contented to take the wool, but they shave hide and all, and some of us are bound to 'em, soul and body. I niver stood in debt to no man yet, but if iver I'd been as much as half a crown behind, I should niver again ha' dared to call my soul my own. Look at us! ' he continued passionately, ' Is there man, woman or child here as can read or write? ' No one stirred in answer to this question. ' Is theer man, woman or child here as can say theer's been bread enough in the house for a month past? Is theer a man here can say he's out o' debt? Is theer a man amongst us as doesn't know in his own heart as he's a slave? What's before us, men and brethren? Sweat and labour, hunger and sickness, and old age for men as has a right to be young for twenty 'ears to come. Labour and little bread, and the Bastile at the end of it, an' a parish grave. I swear here, among my fellow-men. I'll niver rest till I get justice for the men I've lived amongst and worked amongst. I'll neither tek short weight from any fogger nor give long weight, an' I'll buy in open market, wheer I can get best value for my money. I'll do a man's work, but I'll have a man's wage. I'll live like a man, an' when I can do that no longer, I'll die like one.'

He stepped down from the wheel-barrow, still holding the capful of nails in his hand, and taking me by the arm, led me through the throng. I think his grip was a good deal stronger than he fancied, but with the dread his defiance of authority provoked, a certain brightness of exultation mingled, and I was too proud of him to show how much he hurt me.

CHAPTER II

WE were at the foot of Parson's Lane when Mr. Allardyce overtook us at a hasty pace. I had stolen an occasional look at my father on the way, and he had been so stern and pale that I had not dared to speak to him.

'Salter,' said Mr. Allardyce, 'I'm afraid you've brought yourself into trouble by this morning's work.'

'So be it, sir,' said my father.

'What do you mean to do?' Mr. Allardyce asked. 'How do you intend to support yourself and your family?'

'That's as dark to me as it is to you, sir,' said father; and we all walked on in silence for a while. 'The neighbours 'll be staunch wi' me,' father added after this pause, 'and I don't suppose the foggers can tell my nails from another man's. I can place the week's work amongst the neighbours, I dare say.'

'You mustn't do that, Salter,' Mr. Allardyce answered. 'You'll bring your neighbours under the same ban as yourself. How much do you earn a week?'

My father shifted the capful of nails he carried from one hand to another, and stood thoughtfully scratching his head in the middle of the road. Mr. Allardyce, as I remember thinking, looked at him with an expression of anxiety.

'Tek it in and out, the year round,' said my father, 'you might call it nine shillings.'

'Nine shillings, eh?' said Mr. Allardyce, twitching at his lips with his lean fingers. 'Nine shillings? I'm not a rich man, Salter—in point of fact, I'm a very poor one—but I think I could manage that.'

'Manage it, sir?' said father. 'As how?'

'I've known you now,' Mr. Allardyce went on, 'for the last year and a half, and I've gone about a good deal amongst your people. I've been thinking that if a man could be found—a man who knows their ways and their hardships and their speech—a real, whole-souled honest, earnest, man——'

'Yes?' said father, looking up at him as he paused.

'I think,' said Mr. Allardyce, 'that you are the man for that business, Salter. It's time these poor dumb wretches found a voice. It's time they found courage and understanding to face their own condition and put an end to it. Now Salter, say the word.'

Father stood staring at the road with a very serious face.

'I've always looked down on them paid agitator chaps,' he said at last, 'and I shouldn't like to be looked on as one of 'em. Apart from that sir, I've seen a strike amongst the nailers, 'ears an' 'ears ago an' I know what it comes to.'

'A strike's a dreadful thing no doubt,' said the curate, 'but desperate diseases need desperate remedies. If we take this work in hand at all, we must do it wisely. We must touch the public sympathy beforehand; we must let the world know what is going on here. We must set the newspapers to work.'

Father's face was flushed at this and he spoke as if he were talking to a crowd, his voice quite strong and clear.

'Ay sir, that's what I've been wishin' for this an' many a 'ear. Let's have that. Let's turn light on these dark places, and then we can begin to clean 'em.'

Mr. Allardyce thrust his hand into his trousers pocket and pulled out a coin.

'That's the recruiting shilling. Salter. Take it. I enlist you in the name of God and man.'

My father accepted the shilling and put it in his pocket.

'It'll go hard wi' me,' he said, 'before I part wi' that. I'm with ye, sir. I'm theer, heart and soul and body.'

They had stood still to talk, but now they moved on again at so quick a step that I was forced to trot at father's side to keep pace with them. Of course I don't pretend that I have given their conversation word for word, and yet it almost seemed to me, on reading it over, that I had done so. The scene is before me as vividly now as it was at its transaction, and it is not too much to say that I have beheld the faces of the two apostles of the new movement as if they had been in the flesh before me, though they have both been in the grave for years past.

'We must set to work at once,' said Mr. Allardyce. 'My old master at Harrow is on the *Times*. I don't know exactly what position he holds, but it's certainly a place of influence. I shall prepare a plain statement of our case, and ask him to do his best to have it laid before the public.'

'If you do that in your own name, sir,' my father answered, 'you'll raise a pretty ran-dan round your own ears. All the respectable folks are agen us nailers. We're looked on as a shiftless, ignorant, drunken lot, and the common talk about is as we deserve no better than we get.'

'Well, Salter,' said the curate, pulling up suddenly and holding out his hand, 'if one plays at bowls, one must expect to meet with rubbers. I can't strike at other people and expect them not to hit back again. But my blood's been boiling ever since I came here, and now I declare for war. I must get back now, but I'll be down to-morrow with my statement, and we'll go over it together. If I'm wrong in any particular, you can correct me. If I leave out anything of importance, you must remind me of it. And now, remember, we're in the same boat, Salter, and we must pull honestly together.'

'Don't yo' be afeard o' me, Mr. Allardyce,' said father.

They held each other by the hand for the last minute, and now, with a vigorous handshake, and a nod to me, Mr. Allardyce turned away and walked home.

'"We've lighted a torch in England this day,"' said my father speaking much more to himself than to me, '"which by God's grace shall never be put out."'

The words puzzled me at the time, but I recall them clearly now, because he puzzled me still further by saying half a minute afterwards with a bright smile, '"Be of good cheer, Brother Ridley."'

I read the story of the burning of the Bishops four or five years later, but until then I had always supposed that Brother Ridley was a nail-making neighbour of ours who bore that name.

'Just run on wi' this, Jack,' said my father, handing me the capful of nails as we drew near home. 'I'll step in and have a talk with Old Blowhard.'

I ran as hard as my legs would carry me, left the nails on the bed in the front room to avoid mother's questionings, and was out again before my father had reached the first cottage. It was there that Old Blowhard lived. He had gained his nick-name by the asthmatic wheeze with which he spoke. I was keen to know what he would think about the matter, and I entered his little workshop unrebuked, and listened to what went on. I could hear old Blowhard's wheeze even through the blast of the bellows. His wife, his two children, and he were all working at different anvils, with scarce room to move in. The constant clink of hammers would have made conversation impossible for anybody unused to that accompaniment.

'I want a word wi' thee, ode flick,' said my father.

'Tek it,' said Blowhard, plunging his rod into the fire and working at the bellows.

'We'em goin' to get up a bit of a strike.' Father always spoke with a broader accent to men of his own class than he used in talking to educated people like the doctor, or the parson, or the district visitors, who were the only decent people who came our way. 'We'm goin' to get up a bit of a strike,' he said.

'Bin you?' said old Blowhard, swinging round to his little anvil, and raining a shower of tinkling blows on the hot iron. 'Then yo' can count me out on it.'

'Strike?' said his wife, looking up from her work, but hammering with increased dexterity and vigour. 'We've got to strike all day and half night. Thee listen to no such rubbidge, Joe. It's easy to say strike, but who's goin' to fill wer bellies?'

'I mek bold to say,' said my father, 'as theer's no white men i' the world this minute as is trod down like we be.'

'Trew for thee, ode lad,' said Blowhard, wheezing away over his anvil. 'But I'm none for helpin' the thieves to rob us. I'd as lief goo an' play as anyody, but wheer's the grub to come from? I remember the last strike thirty 'ear ago. There was a chap from somewheer—London or Brummagen or somewheer that way—talkin' at Quarrymoor about the rights of man. We'd been at play seven wiks, an' I stood and listened to him with my innards empty. I'd ha' gi'en all my rights o' man for a bit o' tommy.'

'An' this is how the kids is to be dragged up?' said my father.

'Yes,' said Blowhard, 'it is, an' be——to it!'

'They got up a strike fund for the colliers,' said Mrs. Blowhard, —'the colliers, as is ten times better off than we be. Yo' get up a strike fund for we, Jack Salter, an' I'll rest my ode bones glad an' willin'.'

'An' so say all on us,' said Blowhard.

The boy and the girl, working as busily as their parents, and almost dexterously, had paid no heed to this conversation, but had amused each other by an exchange of whispered indecencies, and making faces at each other as they worked. The mother, suddenly detecting this irregularity, caught the boy a goblin clout on the side of the head with a piece of cold iron, and went on with her work with no more ado.

'The fund,' said my father, 'is the first thing to think about. S'posin' we can start a fund, be'st willin' to come out, Blowhard?'

'Yes,' returned Blowhard with some emphasis. 'I'll play as long as the money lasts.'

And this for a long time, was the temper we found everywhere. The wretched people confessed to their own miseries. They knew that they were being robbed in a score of different ways. They knew they were not receiving one half of the real value of their labours, but they had grown up to this abject poverty, and all the robberies which galled them were customs of the trade. They had no spirit and no strength to stand out against them, and after a week or two of entirely futile canvassing, father betook himself to other weapons of warfare.

We were about a mile and a half from Castle Barfield, which was, still is, the great centre of population in that neighbourhood. I had only once or twice seen the High Street, which, with its unbroken row of lamp-posts and its gas-lit shops, was a sort of fairyland.

It was getting late in autumn, and the dusk was drawing in when I ventured one evening, after school, to wander for the first time alone into the town. I had started with no definite intention of going anywhere, but there were a hundred objects of interest to me. Foremost among these was the window of the Museum Tavern, where a brace of stuffed foxes grinned at each other across an artificial tree stump in a long glass case, which was flanked on either side by a bouquet of butterflies, and topped by a bird of Paradise, in other glass cases. Beyond that was the canal, whose dirty, stagnant waters, were iridescent with tar and oil. The tow-path changed sides at the bridge, and the bricks on the top of the bridge were cut into deep furrows by the constant friction of tow-lines.

It was an exciting business to watch the lumbering horses urged into a clumsy gallop, and to see them come plunging up the sloping sideway to the bridge, to see them wheeled and driven down the slope on the opposite side, whilst the heavily-laden boat slid of its own impetus under the archway and appeared miraculously on the other side.

There was a great foundry on the bank of the canal, and forty or fifty yards beyond the bridge were the big iron gates through which we could look and see the puddlers at their work—half-naked figures with wild furnace lights about them. It is long since I saw the sight, but it is just as picturesque in memory now, as it was to my childish eyes. At one furnace, at a given moment, the clay stopper would be taken away, and the blinding molten metal would plunge into its sandy bed, and mark slowly a burning pattern on its darkness, the 'sow', as they called the main channel, giving birth to its litter of pig-iron, and the brilliant device fading from white to red and from red to a dull earthy brown. Then from another furnace one might see the 'bloom' (an incandescent mass of iron) extracted by the aid of enormous tongs, placed upon an iron trolly and swiftly wheeled away to the forge hammer, whose mighty blows sent out showers of sparks and made the very earth vibrate beneath the feet. Then again, the rolls were within sight, and along the polished iron floor the red-hot lines of metal shot and snaked and writhed as if with some furnace life of their own. Altogether, a fascinating place for a boy.

Then, beyond the foundry, rose a hill, from the top of which a fine view of the country was obtainable. Seen from that point of view, the foundry and the town beyond it were sunk in a kind of smoky bowl, the distant rim of which was furnished by the hills of Quarrymoor. The furnace flames leaped up through the grimy air, and the dim scene was perplexed with a very tangle of chimneys, some of which volleyed fire, whilst from the rest came great columns of smoke, drifting madly in windy weather, but on still evenings sending up each a spiral line with a jewelled coronal on top, which took the colour of the low sun as evening clouds do. There on the hill-top the open country lay smiling on either side in such contrast with the dim Gehenna down below as a cherub might make beside a blackamoor. And when the hill was once achieved there was the still distant town to draw one on with its shops and lights, and its knots of loungers, and that evanescent wonder, the passing of the coach from Birmingham to Wolverhampton.

So it chanced, this particular evening in autumn, that I wandered on and on, free of any sort of toil or care, and with a biggish hunk of baker's bread in the pocket of my ragged corduroy jacket against contingencies. I was hungry enough in those days to find fresh bread a delicacy, and as I went I picked off bits from the lump and munched them with serene satisfaction, staring at the cheap sights, and particularly fascinated by the tinman's shop, where everything was in a blaze of gas and polished metal. Then there was the timber-yard, with stacks of fragrant new-sawn deal, and the inscription 'No Thoroughfare' on the gates, to give the place a delightful flavour of the unknown and impenetrable. Further on were the market gates, through the iron bars of which a boy was free to stare at the waste and empty stalls and spaces which were so busy on Saturday nights. Further still there was the waste ground where the rifle galleries used to stand, and where the circus or the wild-beast show hid its splendours at chance holiday times behind a screen of weather-coloured canvas.

I shall never, whilst I remember anything, forget my astonishment at hearing my father's voice as I turned the corner and came upon this waste ground. He was standing in a waggon, and was surrounded by a crowd of, I dare say, five or six hundred people. He had only at that moment arisen, and I heard his first words: 'Fellow-countrymen.' His face was white and strained, and his eyes were unusually bright with excitement; but I remember that his voice had something in its tone which sounded quite majestic and commanding.

I am a man of some education and experience now, and have

had the opportunities of reading and travel, and I have heard public speech in the English tongue pretty nearly everywhere; but I have never met the man who was a greater master of that art than my father. He knew his theme and he knew his people, and he talked the language familiar to his listeners. When he had spoken outside Mr. Sim's house at Quarrymoor, he had had a very different audience to that which he addressed at Barfield. In those days there was a flush in the coal and iron trades. There was no whisper of foreign competition, and the trade-mark on Staffordshire bars and angles carried them all over the world against every rivalry, and the working men were mainly well nourished, and, as a consequence, were vigorous and independent. Only the wretched nailers and chainmakers were ground down. Perhaps the lock-makers of Darlaston were as ill off, but I knew them only by hearsay, whilst for many a year I tasted the bitterness of our own lot, and saw the misery of our neighbours at close hand, and so can speak with authority for ourselves. My father showed the reason for this condition of things in the course of his speech. The nailers and the chain and lock-makers carried on their work at home, and dealt singly with a middle-man, who stood between them and another middle-man. The second middle-man dealt with the retail trade, and so a third middle-man came in. But the trouble was with the first of the trio, who had the man who worked for him, completely at his mercy. In the bigger industries men worked in hundreds, and when the price of their labour was dealt with, they had a united voice. We fought the battle against starvation single-handed.

I had been used to everything, and I had never thought it a hardship that children should be brought up within sound of the clinking little anvil and the roaring bellows. You bear what you are born to, and this is what makes slavery possible. But as my father talked, and set before the crowd the story of a nailer's life from end to end, and pictured the lives of other working men in contrast, my heart caught fire, and young as I was, I turned rebel against the flat injustice which pursued us from birth to death. I was going to say from the cradle to the grave, but not one of us had ever owned a cradle, if we had so much as seen one.

The crowd laughed and cheered boisterously at part of my father's speech, and at other parts it was indignant and sympathetic, and he stepped back into the little host of his supporters on the waggon amid a roar of applause. I have never been so proud in all my life as I was at that moment, and the sensation was all the sweeter and more exhilarating because up till then I had never had any idea of owning anything to be proud of. But the business was not yet over, for while the cheers were still ringing a man broke through the inner ring of people about the waggon, and began to climb the vehicle in a slow, burly fashion which had a kind of dogged and angry force in it. He was greeted with derisive shouts, and when he had gained his place, and turned his sulky pale face on the audience, I saw that it was Mr. Sim. He stretched out a hand to the crowd, as if claiming a hearing, and, after a liberal storm of noise, the folks quieted down and let him have his say. I am willing to admit that, in his own unprepossessing way, he made a dominant figure, with his broad shoulders and his big paunch, and the bulldog look in his face of oil and grime.

'I've been a-listenin', men an' brethren,' began Mr. Sim, 'to the pack o' lies that chap here has been a-stuffin' you up with. I've done business wi' Jack Salter off an' on for twenty year.'

'An' throve on it, aperiently,' said one man in the crowd; and at this there was a laugh. Mr. Sim glared at the interrupter for an instant, but, not being very nimble in his wits, could find no repartee for him. 'Theer's a lot more meat on thy bones,' pursued the man, 'than theer is on t'other chap's.'

This tickled the audience mightily, and, as Mr. Sim lost his temper at their laughter, they laughed the more. My father, though hardy and upright, was small of stature and thin as a lath, and his opponent was like a prize bullock for fatness.

. This chap's known,' said Mr. Sim, sulkily gesticulating at my father and the crowd—' fur an' wide he's known for a land lawyer. He might ha' done as well as any man i' the trade if he'd ha' kep' a civil tongue betwixt his teeth; but he must goo an' quarrel wi' his bread an' butter, and get out o' work. Then he tries to spite them as he never done his duty by, in tellin' a pack o' lies about 'em.' His voice was hoarse and ineffectual, and he was a good deal jeered at; but he stuck to his work with a better pluck than I should have given him credit for. 'Now,' said he, 'I'm a-goin' to ask this here Jack Salter a question. Come out here, Jack Salter.' My father stepped to the front of the waggon and faced him. 'Have you done a hand's turn at your trade this two months?' Mr. Sim demanded of him.

'No,' said my father quietly, 'not one.'

'J'ear that?' asked Mr. Sim. 'Now then. How have you lived that while?—answer me that.'

'I'll answer that,' my father answered, 'with all the pleasure in the world; but I must have Mr. Allardyce's good leave for it first.'

I had not seen Mr. Allardyce until then, but I heard his voice answer from the back of the knot of people on the waggon. I suppose he had been sitting on the ledge, for as he spoke he stood almost head and shoulders above the rest.

'You can have that, Salter, ' he said in his clear and cultured voice.'

'Then, here it is,' said my father: 'The Reverend Mr. Allardyce an' me were talkn' together awhile ago about this honourable an' injured gentleman '—indicating Mr. Sim. 'Anybody as looks at him can see the world has used him cruel hard. He's one of Pharaoh's lean kine, he is. I took him a capful o' nails one day, weighed twice o' purpose for a test. It scaled over seven pound, and when he weighed it he made it scale at five pound fourteen ounce. Well, my friends, I took a bit of liberty with him an' theer. With your good leave, I'll try it on him once again. I told him there wasn't a man in his trade as wasn't a daylight robber. That's strong language, and if it isn't true, an' if it can't be proved, it's vicious language. But it is true, an' he knows it, an' I know it, an' you know it, an' in a wik or two at the outside the whull wide world 'll know it, an' in our time, please God, these fat grinders o' the faces o' the poor 'll be made to pay a fair price for a fair weight, and cease from their extortions. You've asked for the story, Mr. Sim, an', you must tek it as it's in my poor power to tell it.'

Mr. Sim was in a too pronounced minority, and his attempt to silence this denunciation was met with a noise so hostile that he drew back, and listened for what had yet to come with a dreadful scowl upon his face.

'I swore that day,' pursued my father, 'before his face and in the hearin' of all as cared to listen—I swore that day I'd niver rest till I'd got justice for the men I'd lived amongst and worked amongst.

I told him an' them as when I could live no longer like a man, I'd die like one. The Reverend Mr. Allardyce was by, an' we walked a part o' my road home together. Says he to me, " Salter, it's time these poor dumb wretches found a voice," he says. " You're the man to find it for 'em. How much do you earn week in, week out? " I put it at nine shillin'. " It's more than I can afford," says he, " but I'll find that if you can live on it." And with that he puts into my hand a shillin', and says he, " I enlist you in the name of God and man." 'And now my brethren,' cried my father, when the roar of cheers had died away, 'I'm a paid agitator, and Mr. Sim has got the truth out o' my own lips I'm a paid agitator, and between ourselves, it'll be a longish time afore I get as fat on the job as he's grown to be on other folks' labour.'

Mr. Sim climbed down from the waggon, and would have been hustled a good deal if Mr. Allardyce had not leaped down after him. But my father, plain as his words were, had told the story in a splendid heat of passion and triumph, so that it went through his hearers like a fire, and from that hour the parson was a hero.

CHAPTER III

'JACK,' said my father to me early next morning, 'I want thee to run an errand into Barfield. You've got to find out where Mr. Joseph Brambler lives. Anybody 'll tell thee. It's a biggish whitish house on the left-hand side as you mak' for the Barfield Arms.'

'Opposite where thee was speakin' last night?' said I.

He looked at me and laughed.

'Wast thee there?'

I nodded in assent.

'If it hadn't been for Mr. Allardyce,' said my father, 'theer'd ha' been trouble for Mr. Sim, I fancy.'

'I'm none so sure,' said my mother, who was washing the baby before setting about her customary day's work. 'I'm none so sure there won't be trouble for thee, Jack.'

'Trouble for me?' he responded. 'What should bring trouble for me?'

'Ode Blowhard's got some news as some o' the Barfield lads followed Sim as far as Quarrymoor,' said mother. 'They stoned him a great part o' the way, and when he got home they broke his winders.'

Father whistled at hearing this, and drew a rather doubtful forefinger down one bristly cheek, after a fashion he had. Then he laughed.

'I'm none fond of ode Sim,' he said, 'but I should be sorry if damage happened to the man through me. I let him have a rare dressin'-down last night, and that took all the spite out o' me. Let me have a right good say to a man, face to face, and, so far as I am concerned, that's a cure for malice.'

'Ay, ay!' said mother, in a rather scornful assent to this. 'But suppose it's t'other chap as gives thee a tongue wulkin'—how then? Thee hasn't cured Sim's malice, if thee'st cured thine own.'

'Eh, my pretty wench!' said father. 'Sim's like enough to hate me, and, from his point o' view, he's got a cause. A wolf 'll have no likin' for a ship-dog in any case; but if the wolf once had the right to call himself the dog's gaffer, why, he's like to hate him all the more.'

'He'll be makin' some sort of a law business agin thee out on it,' said mother.

'Nay, nay,' returned father. 'I'd naught to do with the breakin' of his windows, nor with the Barfield lads hullin' a pebble or two after him. He might law me for my words, to be sure, but he knows a game worth two o' that. Silence is his best hold, an' he knows that full well.'

'He means to law thee, Jack,' said my mother, sticking to her theme, womanlike.

'Niver thee fret thyself, my pretty wench,' said father.

Mother turned on him angrily.

'I wish thou wouldst not play the fool wi' me, Jack! That's the second time I've been thy "pretty wench" within a minute.'

'Why, lass,' said my father, 'it's not like thee to fly out at a fond word; thee hasn't many of 'em.'

"Say no more, Jack,' mother responded. 'I know I'm a fool to think it, but I can't abide the word, because it sounds as if thee wast scoffin' at me. I'm none of a pretty wench now, whativer I was a dozen years ago.'

'If thou hads a chance to look thy best,' said father 'thou'dst be a pretty wench to-day, Polly.'

He put his arm round her neck and kissed her.

'It's like thy good heart to say so, Jack,' said mother.

'Thou won't be angry at the word again, my pretty wench?' said father.

'Nay,' she answered, laughing. 'Shalt have thy way, thou great gawby! But eh, thou'rt a good man to me Jack.'

'And thou'rt a good wench to me, Polly. And Jack,' said my

father, seeing me staring open-eyed at this scene, 'thou'lt be a good lad to the pair on us—eh? By the time thou'rt grown up to be a man, Jack, we shall be a brace of old 'uns, thy mother and me. She'll want all the love her children can offer her, and well her's arned it. Sweat an' trouble from year's end to year's end, Jack, and no chance of anythin' else till the grave opens; and it's all for thy sake an' mine.'

'Ah, Jack,' said mother, stooping to kiss me, 'thou hast the right to be proud o' thy feyther. There's no man like to him. He's the best man i' the world, be the next wheer he may.'

There were tears in her eyes as she spoke, and I know she meant every word she said. For my own part, I believed her then with all my soul, and I have not very greatly changed my opinion since. We children knew very well how tenderly our parents loved each other, and we had all the more opportunity for making acquaintance with that fact, because our mother had a certain quick tartness of temper, and was constantly being brought back to her normal worship of father by his unfailing patience with her.

'If it wasn't for thee, Jack,' I have often heard her say, 'there's no house in the parish 'ud be fuller o' strife than ourn.'

At this he would always smile, and whatever the cause of war there might have been was knocked on the head. It was an odd thing that we youngsters never got the rough edge of her tongue, though we must have tried her sorely very often. Our row swarmed with children, as the houses of the miserably poor always seem to do, and in comparison with that of our compeers our home-life was elysian. For it was a word and a blow everywhere, and in houses where a thin rod of iron, white-hot at one end, was as likely an instrument of chastisement as any you could think of, the consequences were sometimes pretty ghastly. One little wretch had lost an eye that way, and a good many had seams and scars to show if they had thought them strange and uncommon enough to make a show of them. I look back at the life with a kind of wonder, and my heart aches often to think that little children are leading it at this day. Forty years of civilising influences have done much to abolish the old unthinking brutalities; but the hunger is still there, and the squalor is there, and the black old vista which no ray of hope can pierce is there for most of them. If my father had lived, he might—

God knows—have succeeded in giving all this misery a voice. I think he had the power.

But I am wandering again, and must get back to my story.

'Now, get thee away, Jack' said my father. 'You know who to ask for? '

'Yes,' I answered, 'for Mr. Joseph Brambler.'

'Right! Tell him I'm much obliged, and I'll be theer.'

With this simple message, and instructions to bring back faithfully any answer which might be entrusted to me, I set out. It was Saturday, and therefore a whole holiday from school.

The autumn day was clear, and soft, and warm, and the adventure was altogether delightful. I was filled to the chin with pride at the idea of being sent to so big and fine a house as that inhabited by Mr. Joseph Brambler, and I wondered vaguely enough what it would be like inside, and whether it would be more glorious than Mr. Sim's kitchen.

In that splendid apartment there was a high mantelpiece, shiny with black lead and polish, and surmounted by two great curved shells, two glittering lumps of glass refuse—a common chimney ornament in that part of the country at that time of the day—and four tall brass candlesticks, gleaming with a golden lustre. To my infant fancy, Mr. Sim was rich enough to have had his whole house built of the precious metals, and I associated these brass candlesticks in my mind with those of gold in Solomon's temple.

There was a dresser in Mr. Sim's kitchen, which was rich in valuables in itself, and was surmounted by a plate-rack filled with plates and dishes of various sizes, bespeaking a prodigious prodigality of living. I knew the uses of a plate or a dish when I saw one, but—I speak the plain truth—there was no such thing in my father's house, and never had been. There was a battered old tin trencher, which did duty for all it had to do, and could have borne a heavier duty than it carried. We had in addition two or three tin mugs, a little lidless saucepan, and an old kettle, and these made up the whole *batterie de cuisine* and table furniture, with the exception of a spoon or two, and a few odd-handled knives and forks.

Judging from its size, Mr. Joseph Brambler's house had a right to be as much superior in splendour to Mr. Sim's, as Mr. Sim's was to ours, and I was strongly consious of the social difference which existed between Mr. Joseph Brambler and myself.

When at last, I had covered the two miles or so, and stood at Mr. Joseph Brambler's gate, I was more than half inclined to run away. A little boy was playing in the garden, a boy of about my own age, a celestial boy to my fancy, so far as raiment went, and not at all of the same species with me. He wore a hat shaped like a pot-bellied pitcher turned upside down—a structure of some thin gray stuff, built on an underwork of wire or cane; and this, with a tassel depending on the top of it, fairly crowned him in my eyes. He wore in addition a spotless white pinafore, a pair of very short trousers, white socks, and very shining shoes, which were fastened over the instep with a glittering glass button. The boy is a man now, and a better-hearted yokel does not live; but he goes in awe of me because I write for the newspapers just as I went in awe of him, at the first sight of him, because of his clothes. Seeing me standing at the gate, and looking in with a timorous aspect, he came at me with warlike yell, with his mouth open, as if he were ready to devour me. But seeing that I did not run away, he moderated his pace, and finally stopped at a distance of two or three yards.

'What do yo' want?' he asked, and added without waiting for an answer, 'Go away. Hook it, an' be slippy!'

This, delivered in as broad a local accent as I owned myself, and accompanied by a vulgar facial distortion and a projection of the tongue, brought the boy down from that elysium in which imagination had placed him, and set him on plain earth, as pure and mere a boy as I was.

'I've got a message for Mr. Joseph Brambler,' I said, 'an' I want to see him.'

'Likely story,' said the boy. 'Git out!'

'I shan't!' I answered. 'I've got to see Mr. Joseph Brambler, an' I'm a-gooin' to.'

The boy here took me at a disadvantage, for close to his hand stood a wheelbarrow full of small stones, and taking up a handful of these, he hurled them at me. Most of them were intercepted by the bars of the gate, but some came through, and stung me so sharply that I began instantly to look about for means of retaliation. I was in the act of stooping for a stone, when I heard the gate bang, and thinking that the enemy was upon me, I turned to face him, and ran full into the grip of a very burly man who seized me by the collar of my jacket and bore me ineffectually struggling into the garden.

'Come on,' said my captor; 'come on. I'll pepper you!'

He marched me into the house and landed me half strangled in the hall.

'Now, then,' he continued, dropping me from his grasp as if I had been a kitten or a puppy, 'let's have a look at you.'

He took a look at me, and I took a look at him. If he had not used me somewhat roughly already, I should have seen little enough in his aspect to alarm me. He had a vast flaccid paunch, which looked the bigger because of the flapping dog-eared pockets of his corduroy trousers. He had a great flaccid mouth with a pendulous under lip which showed his lower teeth. His upper teeth, being unusually long and projecting, showed themselves beyond the upper lip. His eyes were large and staring and watery, and his eyebrows, strongly marked and of a dry, sandy colour, were in the middle of a low forehead, so far above the eyes that their position gave him a permanent look of being supremely astonished. He stared hard at me—I staring, I suppose, equally hard at him—and he seemed to be so monstrously amazed at what he saw in me that some reflection of his look must have crept into my own face.

'Ye seem to know what your eyes were made for, *you* do,' said he. 'Is theer anythin' in me to strike a body wonderstruck?'

I said, 'No sir,' and I thought he looked disappointed.

'Oh,' he said, 'there ain't, ain't there?'

I said, 'No sir,' again.

'Well, well,' he said, pettishly, 'you needn't 'arp upon it. What was you a-doin' to my nevew Jeremiar, outside?'

'I was only saying I had a message for Mr. Joseph Brambler, sir.'

'Oh,' he said, 'you've got a message for Mr. Joseph Brambler, have ye? Nothing for Mr. Jeremiar Brambler?'

'No, sir,' I answered, 'only for Mr. Joseph.'

'Ah!' he said, and this time I thought he looked pleased—'*only* for Mr. Joseph.' Then he said aloud, though evidently to himself, 'He feels the difference.' He straightened his vast waistcoat with both hands, and smiled, and his raised eyebrows gave his smile a look of frank incredulity and wonder which was very comical, but very amiable and reassuring at the same time. '*Only* for Mr. Joseph! Very well, my lad,' he continued, after a little smiling pause, 'you'd better wait in here.'

He threw, or rather pushed open a door which faced upon the hall, and passed me into the most gorgeous apartment I had ever seen or dreamed of until then. It is lucky, perhaps, that I can correct my childish impression by others of a much later date, though my present knowledge makes my childish memory look ludicrous beyond the common. The Brambler drawing room is a crowded little apartment, filled in all corners with solid mahogany in horsehair. It is just possible to traverse its narrow and difficult passes without coming into destructive collision with some ugly and useless article of clumsy bric-à-brac. I write of it in the present tense, for I have visited it quite recently, and it has hardly changed a horsehair. This is what it is, but when I think of what it was when I first saw it, and as I figured it to myself years afterwards, I am at a loss for adjectives. I had not conceived and could not have conceived of such a hall of splendour.

I uttered a soft 'Oh!' and stood enraptured, with clasped hands.

Mr. Jeremiah Brambler looked down upon me, smiling, with his eyebrows in the middle of his forehead, as if the world presented him with an astonishing but amusing puzzle.

'Ah, my b'y,' he said, stooping ponderously down to me, 'that strikes you, eh? That's *my* doin's. My arrangemint, that is, both in form and colour. When I came home it was just exactly as I'd left it. Ode oak iverywheer. Ode oak, an' nothin' but ode oak. I brightened it up for 'em.'

I said 'Yes, sir?' in exceeding poverty of spirit, and my inwards were as water because of the chamber's splendour.

'Yes,' he said, ''twas me as done it, and if it hadn't ha' been for me, they'd niver ha' dreamt on it.'

I said 'No sir?' in as complete a trembling, and he beamed all over.

'The very child can see it!' he said aloud to himself, and pulled with both hands at his waistcoat, settling his fat chin in his high collars with a look of self-contentment so complete that I have never seen its like in any other man until this day.

I stood there, twirling my patched little cap in both hands, and lost in wonder and admiration as I was, I can remember that Mr. Jerry Brambler was greatly pleased to have made such an impression upon me.

'I don't expect my brother, Joseph, home this yet awhile,' he said with a fat and smiling condescension. 'I suppose you've got to wait for him?'

I supposed so too, though I did not see why so simple a message as I had to deliver might not have been trusted to his repetition. But I thought he was pleased when I said I had to wait, though by-and-by he took an air of deep musing, standing in an affected posture, with one hand propping an elbow, and the fingers of the other hand caressing his fat shaven cheek, whilst his big head drooped to one side, and his watery grey eyes explored the ceiling and the walls. I sat gaping in complete wonderment at him and his surroundings, and when I thought he had quite forgotten me, he sent a sudden furtive shaft of a glance at me to see if I were looking at him; and seeing that I was, he smiled again, and went on with his posing. All on a sudden he turned as if an idea had suddenly occurred to him, and banged open a piano which stood at one wall of the room. I had never seen a piano at that time, or, so far as I know, heard of one, and when he sat down upon a music stool and cuffed the keys until the instrument fairly shrieked and groaned, I was really very seriously frightened. As to what his performance was really like, I have of course no idea, but I remember being surprised at the sprightly agility with which his big hands walked over the keys at times, and when at moments the storm-cloud of noise severed a little, and something like the beginning of a tune shone through the rift, I thought him really wonderful. What struck me as the most remarkable part of the business was that his hands knew their way about without the aid of his eyes, for during a good half of the time he played he was lolling his chin on his shoulder and smiling at me in an exquisite appreciation of his own skill.

If the admiration and wonder of so simple a listener as myself could please him, he certainly had them in full measure, and he banged and trilled away at the piano, and ogled me and the ceiling and smiled more and more, until it seemed impossible that a human creature could hold more self-contentment. Then as suddenly as he had charged the piano his face clouded. It was like that of a baby who breaks into tears in the middle of a laugh. He closed the lid of the instrument slowly and sadly, and shook his burly head from side to side.

'No, no,' he said in a profoundly mournful voice. 'I shall never be a Don at it. Never.'

Then, without another look at me, he went dejectedly drooping out of the room, and left me to my own amazement.

I stood there alone for a long time, not daring to sit down in such a palace, as I thought it, and growing very weary of the monotony of waiting; but nobody came near me, and I did not hear a sound about the house for at least an hour. In this extremity I made a first unconscious attempt at hypnotism, for the sun happening to shine dazzingly on the brass knob of the room door, I found that by staring hard at it, I could blind myself to everything in the room, and mask the glitter of the door-knob itself by a cloud of warm green light. I think I must have been within an ace of going to sleep over this experiment, when a brisk step in the hall aroused me, and a man came into the room.

'Hillo!' he said in a quick, imperative voice. 'Who are you, and what brings you here, eh?'

I was so dazzled that his face, stooped down until it almost touched my own, went and came before me in alternate pulses of sight and blindness. Now it was there with a strange vividness, and now it was not there at all. This was disconcerting, and I did not answer all at once, so the new-comer, by way of quickening my intelligence, took me by the ear with a sharp pinch of thumb and finger, and repeated his enquiries:

'Who are you, eh? What are you doin' here, eh?'

'Please, sir,' I answered, 'father's sent me on a arrand to Mr. Joseph Brambler.'

'Well,' he said crisply, 'I'm Mr. Joseph Brambler. Who's your father, and what's your arrand?'

'My father's Jack Salter, if you please, sir, and he's very much obliged, and he'll be theer.'

'Good!' said Mr. Joseph Brambler. 'Come this way.'

He turned round as if he worked upon a pivot, and marched straight out of the room, along the hall, and into a paved yard which overlooked a garden. When he reached the door which led to the yard, he turned sharp round the corner, and when, in turn, I reached the corner, he had disappeared as if the earth had swallowed him. But he had only turned very briskly into another doorway, and in a second I heard him calling from it.

Guided by his voice, I found myself in a new apartment, which was in itself another wonderland. There was a burnished meat-hastener before a big, cheerful fire, and there were burnished dish covers hanging on the walls. A rosy girl in a clean cotton print, the sleeves of which left her round red arms bare below the elbow turned to look at me. She had a white cap such as is commonly worn by domestic servants, and looked very bright and clean and tidy.

'Jane,' said Mr. Joseph Brambler, 'gi'e this yiungster a goodish slab o' that cold pie. He looks as if he'd got room for it.'

The girl laughed pleasantly, and gave me a glance of not unfriendly enquiry as she turned to execute her master's order. She disappeared for a moment, and then came back with a big brown earthen dish, a plate, a knife and fork, and a loaf of bread. She arranged these on the table, and, having set a chair before them, smilingly invited me to take a seat.

I obeyed shyly, and the girl, standing over me, took up the knife and fork and cut out a great wedge of the cold meat pie and set it on the plate before me. Then she put the fork in my left hand and the knife in my right, and stood back, a little sideways, in the expectation of seeing me fall to. Mr. Joseph Brambler wore the same look of benevolent expectation, and, between the two of them and my own utter ignorance, I was so embarrased that I felt liker crying than eating, though I had never had set before me a meal which looked a hundredth part as inviting. I knew, of course. that civilized people ate with the aid of knives and forks, but our folks were nailers, and had no use for such gauds. For my own part, I had been reared mainly on plain bread, and not too much of it, and the commonest way of eating it had been to take a hunch in my hand and sop it in weak tea—by way of uncommon luxury—or in water, or milk-and-water. One could not treat the pie in that fashion in the presence of these superior people, and hungry as I was then, and always was, I would much rather that the pie had not been set before me.

'Pitch into it!' cried Mr. Joseph Brambler, standing there very plump and pink, and looking remarkably clean in his white eyebrows and fringe of silver whisker. 'Now let's see how soon you can put away the lot on it.'

I sat there feebly, knife and fork in hand, not knowing how to begin.

'He's shy, master,' said Jane. 'It's we a-starin' at him as puts him off it.'

'Like as not you're right, Jane,' said Mr. Brambler. 'Let him have his fill, anyhow.'

With that he came round the table, patted me encouragingly on the shoulder with an admonition to let fly at it and show what sort of a man I was, and so he walked briskly out of the room and through the yard into the house, his heels tapping on the bricks as he walked with a sound of mingled smartness and authority.

Jane took her place once more behind me, and cut up the wedge of the pie into available pieces, and then, turning away, went about her own morning avocations.

Then, being left to myself and shyness gradually vanishing, and the succulent flavour of the pie reaching my nostrils with a scent more and more ravishing and unendurable, I set to work and made the first meal of my lifetime.

I have sat at good men's boards since then. I have had the good fortune to sit at some rather unusually well-furnished tables, but I have never tasted again anything like that pie. It was myrrh and frankincense to the nostrils, it was heavenly manna to the palate, it was marrow to the tongue. It was a dish celestial, and yet satisfying. Not satisfying all at once, I well remember, but meeting appetite with a *non possumus* as the end of the third wedge began to disappear. What a recollection it is, even now! I had never, never had enough before. It was a glorious, an indescribable experience—a memory unique and unapproachable.

'Poor little divvle!' said Mr. Brambler, when he came back and surveyed the havoc I had made. 'I'll tell thee what it is, young fellow. Theer's many a monarch a-reigning on his throne as'd habdicate this minute for a twist like thine.'

CHAPTER IV

AT this I felt that I blushed right up to the roots of my hair, and began to feel that I had taken an unwarrantable liberty with the pie, though, had I been able to proceed to the last morsel of it, I know that the rosy Jane would have made me welcome, and that her master would have had no reproof for her.

Mr. Brambler, with his hands in his breeches pockets, and his hat cocked on the back of his head and a good deal on one side, stood with his feet far apart, and looked at me with a waggish and friendly air, so that by-and-by I was compelled through all my blushes, to a sheepish grin.

'Now we shall do, eh?' said Mr. Brambler, making a motion as if he were going to sit down upon nothing, and straightening himself again. 'All right now, eh?'

I said 'Yes, sir,' and he laughed with a rich enjoying chuckle.

'Now, I suppose,' he said, 'that you never had a tuck-in like that in all your life afore, did you?'

'No, sir.'

'Never, I'll be bound,' said Mr. Brambler. 'It's the first, but it needn't be the last. You can come in here, through the back way, any time you're passin', and Jane'll have a bit of a pickin' for you of some sort or other.'

This opened up such a unheard-of prospect that I hardly know whether I felt more gladness or wonder.

'I shan't expect you to be in an' out o' the house all day and every day,' said Mr. Brambler. 'But when you're passin'—say two or three times a week.'

I said that he was very kind in some clumsy fashion, and I wondered at my luck, and wished I could share it with my mother.

'I'll teach that blackguard a lesson,' said Mr. Brambler addressing Jane. 'He had the cheek to stand afore me an' defy me. I'll be even with him! I'll Sim him afore I've done with him!'

'I'm glad you've took up your parable agen him, master,' said Jane. 'My bringin'-up was Quarrymoor, though I was in a daycent farm-house, an' had nothin' to do with the poor nailers. But I've known that Sim from my childhood uppards, an' allays knowed him for a bitter hard 'un.'

'He's all that,' assented Mr. Brambler, 'and I'll make him pay for his cheek to me afore I've done with him.'

From all this, and much more to the same effect which followed it, I learned that Mr. Sim had somehow insulted Mr. Joseph Brambler and that one of Mr. Brambler's ways of being revenged upon Mr. Sim was to show me kindness.

I am sure that in my heart I hoped that the quarrel between them might never be patched up, and I dare say that a good many of my seniors, who would have told me that my wish was unchristian, would have felt it quite as stongly if they had been situated as I was. I was too poor to feel affronted at the thought of charity, and not old enough to know a great deal about honourable pride; but I had eaten the only real meal of my lifetime, and others of an equal volume and quality lay before me, and the prospect was quite agreeable enough to go on with.

I was put under examination as to my educational acquirements by Mr. Brambler, who was so surprised at my proficiency that he patted my head and gave me sixpence before he dismissed me.

Under this knockdown blow of wealth and pride I staggered home, and there related all that had befallen me. My mother cried at my description of the meal, and wiped her eyes with her poor cinder-blackened, herden apron.

'Ah, Jack,' she said, 'if thy fayther and me could ha' got 'em for thee, thee shoudst niver ha' gone short o' thy victuals—thee nor none on thee, nayther.'

'It's a hard fight, lass,' said father, 'but you've fowt it bravely, an' please God, we'll go on fightin' it.'

I can understand it better now, but I was too young and ignorant to do anything just then but wonder at my mother's tears over the fact that I had a hearty meal for once in a way. But I learned afterwards that my visits to Mr. Brambler's house were a sore trial to her pride. She might have done better than she had. There was a young 'shingler' at the big foundry who would have married her years ago if she would have said the word, and she could have enjoyed an income of perhaps thirty shillings per week, and have been free of all but womanly household labour, and in a loyal way she remembered it. In a disloyal way I am sure she never did—no, not for a single instant of her bitter and laborious life.

Mr. Joseph Brambler, I came to learn, had been a noted advocate of the Truck Act, and had given evidence in its favour before a Royal Commission. He was one of the largest wholesale dealers in the nail trade, and he bought from the 'foggers,' who bought from working men like my father. He had allowed it to be known for years that he would buy from any workman at a fair price, and the whole body of men would have been delighted at the chance to deal with him.

But then the poor wretches were tied to the smaller dealers, who fleeced them right and left. They were in debt, and they were absolutely at the fogger's mercy—so absolutely that even when a fair wage was offered them they were unable to take advantage of it, and were compelled to go in the old soul-grinding way. They were the white slaves of England, and there is the truth in a phrase. In America, before the national disgrace and crime of negro slavery brought about its own penalty and worked itself to a solution, amidst all the horror and terror of civil war, it used to be argued very often that the stories of cruelty which were charged against slave-owners were obviously exaggerated or untrue, because no man would be such a fool as to destroy his own property. That theory was proved false in a hundred thousand cases, but even if there had been a Gospel truth in it, it would not have worked in our case.

For when the fogger had killed his white slave—and he did it daily and yearly by exaction and overwork and every possible sort of pretty chicanery—he lost nothing by it. He owned his white slave, owned him soul and body, but he paid nothing for him to begin with, and when he died he had sucked the last drop of profit out of him. That was all.

But just hereabouts in the history a very cruel and terrible thing happened, which I must relate as well as I remember it.

The Reverend Thomas Harper, Incumbent of Quarrymoor, was dead against the movement on which my father and Mr. Allardyce had embarked on together. Mr. Allardyce, though he was poor enough, was a gentleman, and had very high connections in a distant part of the country. I knew later on that his mother was a lady—an Honourable Miss Somebody—and that she had married a clergyman against the wishes of her parents. They had refused to have anything to do with her after this ill-advised union. She seems to have lived an unhappy life, and to have died early. But Mr. Allardyce's grand-father was still living, and the Reverend Thomas knew that he was a nobleman of great estates, and when the curate came to Quarrymoor, the talk was that Mr. Harper would do anything for Mr. Allardyce, and that he looked through his influence to secure a fat living somewhere. Then, when it came out that Mr. Allardyce and his lordly grandfather had never so much as exchanged a word with each other, the Incumbent began to treat his curate as if he had been guilty of false pretences, and to do his little best to spite him, and to thwart his plans, as people of petty nature will in such a case.

Mr. Allardyce seems to have borne it all patiently, for the sake of the people amongst whom he worked and amongst whom he had hoped to spend his life, and the Incumbent made it his business to force a quarrel with him. So much pretty nearly everybody knew, though, of course, there was no end of imaginative tags and odds and ends of lies and conjectures with which to embroider the story.

In the Black Country, the familiar form of Thomas is Tummy, and Tummy stands in turn for 'paunch,' and Mr. Harper being a man of gross habit of body, was disrespectfully known everywhere as the Reverend Tummy. He was a short, fat, greasy man, and poor as we all were, we knew very well that the Reverend Tummy was not a gentleman, as Mr. Allardyce was. The poor and ignorant are a good deal quicker and keener at that sort of discovery than imposters in this line of fancy. They know a gentleman when they see one, and they go through the counterfeit like a gimlet.

Well, Mr. Allardyce had been down to our wretched little house time and time again, concocting with my father the letter which was to go to the *Times*. He had read aloud to my father a letter from that old college friend of his who was now associated with the great journal, and the upshot of the letter was that, if Mr. Allardyce would make a plain and unprejudiced statement of the case, it would certainly be printed. The case was prepared, and prepared with a good deal of labour, for Mr. Allardyce had determined not only to send a statement which would draw public attention to the facts, but to back it up with information so detailed and precise that the *Times* authorities might send down a commissioner so armed that in a day or two he could verify circumstances adduced.

This was not meant for publication, but it gave five times as much trouble, and took five times as much to get ready, as the letter itself.

When all was ready there was a final reading, and I shall never forget the scene. Mr. Allardyce sat in our one chair reading by the light of a tallow candle. My mother sat on the bed, and my father stood beyond the table with a grave, attentive face.

As for me, I was tucked up on my little heap of shavings, with a sack drawn up to my chin, and ears and eyes both wide open.

The letter as it appeared is in my possession now. It is written in a sort of grave, dry eloquence, and would, I think, carry conviction with it to any open and honest mind.

We, who were amongst the sufferers, whose cause it pleaded, knew the truth of every word, and I know I cried at parts of it in which our condition was unsparingly described.

'That's a true word, sir,' my mother would say at intervals from her place upon the bed.

My father said nothing until the reading was over, but stood with downcast eyes drinking in every syllable.

'Thank you, sir,' he said at last, when the curate laid the manuscript down. 'That's a cry as should ring through England from one end of it to the other. It's the first chance we ever had of makin' our sufferin's known.'

'I hope it may serve its turn,' said Mr. Allardyce, very quietly and seriously, but I could see by his eyes that he was more excited and moved than any of us. 'We have put our hands to the plough, Salter, and there must be no turning back.'

'There's none for me, sir,' said my father, 'even if I wanted it. And I know there's none for you, sir.'

'No,' said Mr. Allardyce, 'there is none for me.'

'I beg your pardon, sir,' said father, 'but I hear as you've got Parson Harper agen you.'

'I would rather not talk of that, Salter,' said Mr. Allardyce, 'even with you. It is quite certain that Mr. Harper will do nothing to help us.' He smiled with a look of humour, and added: 'A Churchman is just as much bound to stick up for discipline as a soldier is, and Mr. Harper, you know, is my superior officer.'

'Well, sir,' said father, 'at least there's no harm in wishing that no trouble may come out of your part in the matter. You're doin' God's work, sir, if ever a man took it in hand i' this world.'

'I know that, Salter,' said Mr. Allardyce, 'and we can do no better than kneel down and ask God's blessing on it.'

He knelt down on the beaten earth floor, and my father and mother imitated his example. He prayed, in simple words which even I could understand, that God would prosper the work which was then begun, and that all bitterness might be kept out of it, and all self-seeking; and that the eyes of men should be opened that they might see, and the hearts of men be softened that they might feel the cruelty and bitterness of the lot of these poor souls, the noise of whose ceaseless labour was even then tinkling in the air about us. It was all so simple and manly and unaffected, it was such a grave and yearning call from a noble human heart, that my mother was moved to open weeping by it; and when they all rose from their knees, I could see my father's eyes glinting wet in the beams of the candle.

I remember to have spoken once or twice of my mother shedding tears, but I would not have anybody believe of her that she was a crying woman. Her courage is the one thing I remember best of her, and when I think of how little she had in all her life that should of right belong to every woman, and remember as I do, and shall do always, how rarely she complained, I am filled with a constant admiration of her fortitude.

Only four days after this, Mr. Allardyce came down in splendid excitement with a copy of the *Times* in which the letter had appeared in full. It was read all over again, and my father beat up all the workers in our row and read it out to them when Mr. Allardyce had gone.

'The Govament 'll tek no notice on it,' said one.

'It was all showed up as clear as that when they stopped the tommy shops,' said another.

'A ——— lot o' good that 'll do we!' said Old Blowhard, and so they all went back to their work again, as unmoved a set of human sheep as ever I saw in my lifetime.

The very next Saturday that came, my father had gone out on some business connected with his new trade of agitator, and mother and I were left alone. I was sedulously practising the art of writing by the help of a pencil and a slate (for, young as I was, I had made up my mind that if any effort of mine could help do it, neither I nor my parents should remain always where we were), when my mother bade me run to a neighbour and borrow a bundle o' rods.

The baby's frock was in unmendable tatters, and she was bent on earning a sixpence or so to replace it, so as not to come upon that allowance of nine shillings a week which my father received from Mr. Allardyce. She had not worked much at the little anvil since father had entered on his new business, but had taken industriously to her needle, and had patched us all, and had taken to the washtub and washed us all, until our shabby and dirty duds were almost respectable to look at. Now and again she had turned to at the old work—for she was a woman who could not bear to be idle.

I got up and ran off to obey her behest, and, being willingly supplied, I carried the rods to our own cottage and took them in by the back way, where, in a little while, mother set to work at them. The little bellows were in full blast, and the little hammer was clinking in the way which had been familiar to me from the very earliest hour of my memory, when the door was thrown open after a brief imperative knock, and in walked the Reverend Mr. Harper. Of course I knew him by sight and name, but he had never darkened our doors until that moment, and I was a good deal surprised to see him. I rose up with the slate in my hand and the pencil in the other, expectant of I know not what; but I fancy that some mischief in connection with Mr. Allardyce was in my mind, and I thought the parson came as an enemy.

There are ways and ways of being fat, just as there are ways and ways of being and doing anything, and Mr. Harper's way was gross and obtrusive, and, to a lean and hungry boy as I was, offensive. He had hard eyes and a loose, sensual mouth, and the very glance he gave me bullied me and awed me and made me hate him rebelliously all at once. Mr. Allardyce was our angel, and this man hated him. Mr. Allardyce was trying to help us, and this man was trying to thwart him and to keep us down. These facts were enough for me.

He turned on the threshold, and beckoned to somebody outside, and a gentleman with a clean-shaven face and reddish hair came in raising his hat as he entered, and standing bare-headed through what followed.

'John Salter lives here,' said Mr. Harper, and I nodding in answer, he asked, 'Where is he?'

'Father's out, sir,' I said.

'Father's out, is he? Ho, ho! Father's out?'

He put up a hand, as if to enjoin silence, and then he made a motion with it to the door which communicated with the other room. The asthmatic wheeze of the bellows and the tinkle of the hammer sounded for half a minute before he broke silence again.

'Who's working there?' he asked.

I answered, 'Mother.'

'Ho, ho!' he said again, and turned with an explanatory air upon his companion. 'Father's out, you observe, and mother's working.'

The stranger looked at me and beckoned me towards him, but as I advanced Mr. Harper intervened between us.

'Leave him to me,' he said; 'you may question him afterwards. Does your father work at his trade at all now?'

I was only a child, but my wits were sharp enough to tell me that he wanted to trap me.

'Father works for Mr. Allardyce now, sir,' I answered.

'Oh!' he said, looking angrily at me. 'And where does father work for Mr. Allardyce? And what does father do for Mr. Allardyce?'

'He doesn't work at home, sir,' I said. 'He works for Mr. Allardyce.'

When father would come home at night, he would stumble on to the bed and sit there in sheer fatigue without a word until my mother would question him; and many a time I had heard him say that he had harder work than nail-making on hand.

'Mr. Allardyce,' said the parson, 'is a very well-meaning and a very enthusiastic young man. It is he who has got up this agitation and this man Salter is his paid agitator. When he knows the country as well as I do, he will perhaps regret his precipitancy.'

'But come, sir,' said the stranger, who, in spite of a marked quietude of manner, spoke with a certain authority—'come, sir. Surely this wants mending.' He waved his hand about the room.

'No doubt, no doubt!' said Mr. Harper with a burlesque of geniality which was patent even to me. 'But who is to mend it if not the men themselves?'

'When will your father be home, my boy?' the stranger asked me.

'I don't know, sir,' I responded. 'He's pretty often very late, sir.'

I put that in to show how hard he worked, but Mr. Harper twisted it.

'You see,' he said—'you see.'

'I don't know that I see,' said the stranger somewhat sharply. 'But I mean to see.'

'My dear sir!' said the parson, and, bowing, drew on one side.

'Your mother is in here, my boy?' the stranger asked me. 'Just say that I should like to speak to her.'

I opened the door, and he followed almost at my heel, and by-and-by he and mother were at talk together. I wanted to hear what was said, but Mr. Harper got hold of me and made me uncomfortable with questions for some ten minutes.

He wanted to know why I didn't go to church, for one thing; and when I told him that I didn't know, he feigned to be terribly grieved. He knew well enough that we had no clothes which were fit to go in and he knew well enough, besides, that I should have been warned off by the beadle if I had any inclination to go—but he played his part even to a baby. He said it was sad, very sad, and I knew he was a humbug and cared nothing at all about it in his heart.

But suddenly, when my society or his own began to pall upon him, he walked into the back kitchen, and greeted my mother with a lordly: 'Well, Mary Salter, and how are you?'

And my mother, looking on him with disdain, responded that she was none the better for his asking the question.

'My good woman—— ' said Mr. Harper, but he got no further.

My mother was not a lady, but she was a decent woman, and I never in my life heard a coarse expression from her lips, yet she turned on that sham servant of the Church, and gave him such a lashing with her tongue that at last he fairly ran to escape her.

'What brings thee i' my house, Greasy Tommy? ' she asked him at last. 'It's the first time you've iver come here sence you come to the parish ten 'ear ago, an' wi' my good will, it'll be the last. Goo an' sit down to dinner wi' the fat foggers as clams wer bellies and sucks wer blood.'

But he was gone, and the stranger had gone with him. Neither of them ever came back again, and my mother's outbreak did us dreadful and unexpected damage. For the strange gentleman was the *Times* commissioner, and he came out with half a column of satiric humour which blighted my poor old father like a hot iron. 'Father's out, and mother's working,' became a byword. It rang cruelly in our ears until the very day of his death. He had to face it on a hundred platforms. He had to face it in the street. It lived with him wherever he went. 'Father's out, and mother's working,' was thrown at me until I was as mad at it as a bull at a red rag, and many a black eye and bloody nose were the fruit of it before it was forgotten. For, by some misapprehension of the writer's, it was to me, and not to the parson—who had really spoken them—that the words were attributed.

That was the first disaster in the campaign. My father was stamped as an idler who left his wife to work at home, whilst he loafed in pursuit of pleasure, and there were leading articles in the newspapers about 'this man Salter,' who posed as the emancipator of his class, and played the lazy tyrant in his own home. God knows how false it was, and He knows, too, how hot and passionate were the tears I shed to have him so maligned. But my father went his way through it all, like an Englishman, and lived to make me prouder of him than if he had been a king.

CHAPTER V

AUTUMN was with us. We were well into the middle of October, and my small legs had carried me from home to Quarrymoor, and from Quarrymoor on to Brays Horton, and from Brays Horton into a country district utterly unknown to me. This was on a Sunday, a day on which my movements were entirely unrestricted. Anybody who knows that land of sludge and smoke and grime, which men call the Black Country, knows how its beautiful borderland smiles by contrast. In a quiet way there is no more beautiful landscape in the world than I can find within ten miles of perpetual smoke and fire, and very much nearer than that there are stretches of pastoral land, and nooks of quiet greenery, and stealing stream, and parcel-shadowed lane, which will vie with anything all our rich England over. I had a great love of Nature as a child, and the quiet, slow changing grays of the sky, and the alternation of lane and meadow, and, more than all, an alluring enchantment of mystery in the dim half-seen hills, drew me on until it was close on mid-day.

The sun was uncommonly powerful for this season of the year, and by this time I was fairly tired, and hungry enough to be ready for the onion and the hunch of bread I carried in my jacket pockets. I stopped in the shadow of a great tree by the side of a little mossy spring, and there, with my toes pushing hither and thither amongst the rustling crisp leaves, I ate my meal and washed it down with a draught from the spring. The warmth of the day had brought out a tribe of belated insects, and they went humming idly with a soothing music. The sky was exquisitely dappled, and it was a treat to lie back, well fed and content, and to stare at it through the masses of transparent red and yellow that hung so silent and motionless overhead.

In the depth of my comfort I fell asleep, and in my sleep I dreamed that Old Blowhard was quarrelling with my father and was threatening him. The dream woke me, and close to me, but hidden by the hedge between us, men were talking. Amongst the voices was one of a man with a cleft palate, who made up for the indistinctness with which he spoke by the noise he made. He was trying, so it seemed, to shout the others down, but at last one of his companions broke out upon him with a torrent of oaths, and ordered him to be quiet.

'We'n took a gaäm in hond,' this man said, when by dint of noisy cursing he had secured silence—'we'n took a gaäm in hond as it's best to be quiet about.'

'Theers nobody within a mile on us,' said a third man.

Then Old Blowhard spoke.

'That's as may be,' he said; 'but, any way, least said, soonest mended.'

Old Blowhard was there, then, I thought, and wondered what should have made me dream that he was threatening my father.

'Well, look here, lads,' said the man with the cleft palate, 'this is what I want to get at. I'm mistrustin' that ode ——— of a Sim, an' I'll ha' nothin' to do with it till I see the colour of his munney.'

'Nor me nayther,' said Blowhard. 'There's no risk in it, as far as I can see, but I've got no spite agen the man, an' I'm d——d if I lay a hond on him without I'm paid for it.'

'That's what I say,' broke in another man, who had not spoken until now. 'Money down afore the work's done.'

I remember this conversation quite clearly, and it must have had some sort of impressiveness at the time. I do not quite remember what I thought about it, but I was certainly miles away from grasping its real significance. Mr. Sim was to pay the men for doing something, and they were determined to be paid beforehand, for fear he should cheat them. I think I had, in addition to this, a dim idea of mischief meant to somebody, but I am not sure that this is not an afterthought.

There was a striking of matches and a lighting of pipes among the men, and then a move was made, at Old Blowhard's suggestion, and they all wandered off along the field. In awhile I took a farewell drink at the spring, and set off towards home, being warned by the changing light that I had all I could do to make Quarrymoor whilst day lasted. From Quarrymoor to my father's cottage every pebble in the road was familiar to me, and I could have made my way blindfold.

I had got no further than the beginning of the scattered street of Brays Horton, when I saw Old Blowhard, and, as I conjectured, the four men who had been talking with him a couple of hours before. Just as I saw him he caught sight of me, and came panting and wheezing across the road to take me by the shoulder. I waited for him without fear, for the man had never done or hinted harm to me, and I was surprised, as well as hurt, by the savage force of the grip he laid upon me.

'Wheirst thou been, young limb o' Satan?' he asked me, bending his pale, grimed face into mine.

I told him, flinching under his fierce hold, that I had been for a walk.

'Whither away?' he asked, gripping me harder still, and shaking me a little.

I don't know what prompted me to it, unless it were my new fear of him, but I told him a lie, and indicated a district quite far from the one I had really visited. I did not know the names of any of the places which lay beyond Bray's Norton, but I pointed wide of the road I had taken, and said I had been over there.

'Oh!' he said, and released me, and walked back to his companions.

He took a reluctant sideways sort of gait, and kept an eye upon me as he crossed the street. When he rejoined his comrades, he said something to them, and with one consent they all turned and stared at me, as I stood rubbing my hurt shoulder in the middle of the roadway. There was some low-toned talk among them, and Old Blowhard pointed in the direction in which I had pointed, and they all looked that way, and then all looked at me again. Then, with rounded shoulders, and their hands plunged deep in their pockets, they lounged away, and I followed at a little distance, afraid to pass them on the road. In a little while, however, they turned into the fields, and then I scurried off in the gathering dusk as fast as my feet would carry me, feeling somehow afraid of the coming night, and the loneliness of it.

I was in the very act of passing the house in which Mr. Allardyce had lodgings, when I met my father, who stopped me and questioned me as to where I had been. Mr. Allardyce came to the door and interrupted the questioning.

'Come in, Salter,' he said. 'We can have but little time together for I have to conduct evening service.'

'You won't be able to be with us, sir?' my father asked in a disappointed voice.

'No,' Mr. Allardyce answered with a smile. 'Mr. Harper has sent down word that he is indisposed.'

'Ah!' said my father. 'He'll have heard about the meetin'.'

'I dare say,' the curate responded, still smiling. 'But come in. Bring your boy with you. You have had a long walk, little man.'

My father made some demur, but Mr. Allardyce insisting, I went into the house, and sat on a chair in a corner, nursing my cap and staring at the lamp and the piano, and the pictures on the walls, and the delicate little china tea-service on the table. It was quite a simple cottage room in itself, but I felt it was more truly a gentleman's apartment than any I had ever seen before. How I knew that I didn't know, but I did know it, just as well as I knew that Mr. Allardyce was a gentleman, and that Mr. Harper was not.

'You'll hold that meeting all the same,' said Mr. Allardyce, 'and if it should last until service is over, I will come round and join you.'

The decent woman who attended to him came in with the tea, and bustled about him with an evident pride and affection.

'Now, master, if thee beest goin' to prache to-night, you must have summat inside you. John Salter 'll tell you that. When ourn was alive, he was a don at the trombone-playin', an' he used to say, theer was nothin' like blowin' to mek a mon faint an' hungry. I'm sure it's the same with prachin'. There's a lot o' wind throwed away in prachin' a sermon in a big waste of a buildin' like our parish church.'

Mr. Allardyce laughed.

'I'm afraid there is,' said he.

'Ah,' said the woman with an answering laugh, 'but you twist a body's words so. Anny road, I've biled a egg, and I've cut a nice thin slice o' cold ham, and you must manage 'em somehow. He'd starve himself to death if he was let to do it,' she added, turning to my father.

'Well,' said Mr. Allardyce, 'I'll eat this evening to oblige you. Now, tell me. Salter, how is this cause going on?'

They talked together, whilst Mr. Allardyce sipped at his tea and trifled with the meal before him. My father sat at table with him, drinking tea from a delicate little cup, which looked strange in his labour-hardened hand, and I, not being supposed to have arrived at an age at which to be trusted with such valuables, had a bowl given me with a liberal supply of hot tea and cream, the same being well sweetened with the first lump-sugar of my experience, and the whole being as glorious a revelation in the way of beverages as Mr. Joseph Brambler's meat-pie had been among edibles.

My father's account of things was not very encouraging, but he had got perhaps a score of children on the school list, who had never been there before, and had permanent help for the parents who dispensed with their services in the home workshop. But he reported that the children were constantly kept from school to work at home, and the stipend intended for their subsistence spent in drink. There was a little zeal for better things among the women, here and there, but the men were sunk in apathy.

'Well, well,' said Mr. Allardyce, 'we are making a beginning. Men who can read and write, and have been taught to think, are not likely to live such lives as their fathers have lived before them. It is enough for us to sow the seed. The more I live, Salter, the more I am convinced of this one thing. There is no wasting honest work. God will never have that thrown away. We can only do our duty, and trust the result to Him.'

'That's so, sir,' said my father.

The bells of the parish church had been clanging close at hand during the progress of the meal, but now they stopped suddenly, and a single bell began to strike a measured note.

'I must go,' said the curate, 'and I will get to your meeting if I can.'

With that he dashed upstairs, and, returning in a moment, took up his felt hat, and opened the door, which gave immediately upon the street. We all three went out together, my father holding my hand in his. The curate, with a parting word, swung off quickly towards the church, and my father led me in the opposite direction to a cottage, in the window of which a solitary candle gleamed on the mist of the autumn night. Perhaps a score of men were lounging about outside, but at my father's appearance there was a general move towards the door, and in a minute the small room in which the meeting was to be held was crowded. There was an old Primitive Methodist there, who insisted on opening the proceedings with a prayer. He encountered some opposition, but conquered in the end; and when his petition was closed my father began to talk to the meeting.

I have often thought that there is something very strange in a child's recollection of the events which stand out in its calendar. There are whole months of which he can recall nothing, and that long after observation and memory are strong and well developed. Then, standing above and between these gulfs of dead oblivion, there are passages of life which are seen so clearly that they might even now be standing before us in broad sunshine. It is thus with me when I recall that day. I see its most trifling incident. I should know again, if I could see them, the rugged faces in the candle-light. My eye travels over them again exactly as if they were before me. I hear my father's voice, and I could almost report his words. The night itself I have cause to remember, and it is impossible that its main incident should fade; but why all the details of the day that went before it should be thus burned as it were, into my mind, I have no power to tell. It is so, and not in this case alone, but in a score of crucial cases in my own experience.

The conference was long, and once or twice it grew stormy.

'All very well for thee, Jack Salter,' cried one man; 'thee'st got thy nine bob a week, whether thee bist at play or at work. It's different wi' wee.'

There was no sense of fairness or of justice. How should there be? But my father worked harder and fared harder than any one of them, and whatever he did was for their sakes. They could not see it, and the main feelings he excited in their minds were those of envy and hatred.

He pleaded with them, wrestled, argued, worked the whole battery of persuasion. It was all of no avail.

'D'ye mean to be a set o' speritless, down-trod slaves all your lives? ' he asked.

'Keep a civil tongue, Jack Salter.'

'Lads! lads! Think o' your wives an' chidren.'

'Think o' your own. Whose missis is it as works, while her mon's at play? '

'At play! ' my father echoed. 'Is it play to walk thirty miles a day on a half-empty belly? Is this play, d'ye think? Try it lads. Break your heart and grind your soul day by day an' hour by hour agen dull stupidity and hard ingratitude, and you'll find out what the play's like.'

This brought the whole crowd up storming, and no wonder. But I know what heart-felt misery my father must have endured before his patience broke in that way, and anger so far got the better of good policy. I believe he would have been ill used among them if Mr. Allardyce had not come in at the instant. His coming calmed the storm a little, but so far as the creation of any purpose went the gathering was a total failure, and my father went away from it dispirited and drooping. Mr. Allardyce walked a mile with us on our homeward way, and tried to cheer him.

No discouragement, Salter! No turning back! No breaking down! The devil has been whispering at me this three months past: "Useless! Hopeless! Give it up! " But it isn't useless, Salter, and it isn't hopeless, and we won't give it up! '

'NO,' said father. 'There's no giving it up while life lasts—but it's a bitter business.'

The words were scarcely spoken, when two or three shadowy figures leapt out of the hedge on either side of the road, and there was a loud cry from Mr. Allardyce. The night was thick with mist, but there was a faint and uncertain light from the full moon, and in it I could see a desperate struggle going on.

'Get to my back, Salter! ' cried the curate, and my father obeyed his bidding, but the five or six assailants were armed with heavy bludgeons, and closed in on all sides at once.

I tore my throat with shrieks, and clung with all my puny strength to one ruffian's legs, until a blow fell to my head, and in a sudden dazzle and crackle of sparks the whole scene went out. But hurried as it was, and maddened as I had been by terror, surprise and rage, I heard Old Blowhard's wheezy breathing, and I knew the voice of the man with the cleft palate when he drew back, with a curse, from a blow dealt him full in the face by Mr. Allardyce. As to how the fight went on, of course I know nothing.

When I came to myself everything was very still and quiet. I was looking up at the naked branches of a tree in the hedgerow, and when I moved there was a rustle of leaves about me. My head ached rather badly, but I was conscious of no other pain. I sat up and listened with all my might, but at first the only sounds I heard were those of my own breathing and the crackling motion of the dead leaves about me. Then, for a moment, there came upon the wind, the sound of a far-off horse's footfall and the hum of some vehicle as it went, skidded, downhill.

At first I had no definite idea of what had happened, but my ideas were gradually growing clearer when a low groan brought everything back to mind with a rush, and I scrambled to my feet, and looked about me. Not a sign I could see either of my father or Mr. Allardyce, but I found a cap in the road, and, scarce knowing what I did, I put it in my pocket.

A dreadful terror of the silence and the night was laying hold upon me when I heard that low groan repeated, and running to the dry ditch at the roadside, I saw a pale blot of something in the darkness, and kneeling down to look at it nearer, I made it out for the face of Mr. Allardyce. There were dark marks across it, and I shuddered to think what they might mean.

A strangling hand seemed to take me by the throat, and my head swam badly. I was afraid of swooning off again, and I fought against these sensations as well as I could. They gave way in time, and I scrambled down into the ditch, and made such a baby effort as I could to lift the injured man. He groaned a third time as I tugged at his neck with both my hands beneath it, but I could not move him by an inch. I sickened all over when my hands came away damp and sticky with blood, but just then I heard another groan, and there, only a yard or two away, was another pale blot of a face, which turned out to be my father's.

I knelt over him in an agony of pity and fear, and began to cry with sobs which shook my body from head to foot. I tried to raise him as I tried to raise Mr. Allardyce, but with just as little effect. But presently his eyes opened and he looked up at me.

'That thee, Jack?' he said in a whisper. 'I'm afeard they've done for parson.'

'No,' I said; 'he's here.'

Father made an effort to raise himself, but fell back helplessly. 'Jack,' he said, 'thou must keep thy wits about thee, lad. The nighest policeman and the nighest doctor's Quarrymoor.' He panted in his speech, and spoke as if every word were a pain to him. 'Do somethin' to mek sure o' where we be, an' then run for it. Here! leave thy coat i' the middle of the road. There'll likely be none passin' the road at this hour o' the night. Now run. Fetch doctor an' police.'

I needed no second bidding, and I ran with all my speed. The scalded tears tasted salt on my lips, and the bitter sobs so choked me that I had to stop again and again; but at last I reached the doctor's bell and tugged at it until it answered with a peal which frightened me.

A groom came to the gate with a lantern. He was in a state of high ill-humour, but when my panting breath gave me a chance to tell him what was the matter, he dashed into the house and reported to his employer. Then there was a hurry and a bustle, in which a servant girl was sent to run for a policeman—Quarrymoor had but one at that time—and the groom and the doctor harnessed the trap together. The doctor's wife stood on the back steps of the house, and screamed across the stable-yard:

'Bobby!'

'Hillo!' cried the doctor, tugging at a trace-buckle.

'Instrument case?'

'Yes.'

'Lint and bandages?'

'Yes.'

'Chloroform?'

'Yes, yes, yes! Regular mining-disaster fit-out.'

The things required were at hand in a minute, the doctor was in the dog-cart with me beside him, the gates were thrown open and we were in the street.

'That you, Wilkins?'

'Yes, sir.'

'Jump up. Here's a case of murder, I'm afraid, from what this little fellow tells me. That meddlesome chap, Jack Salter, has been set on. He had Mr. Allardyce with him, worse luck, and he's been hammered senseless.'

'Safest not to meddle with these chaps, sir,' said the officer.

'They're very unked if you cross 'em.'

'Keep your eyes about you, my lad,' said the doctor. 'Stop us at the right place. Get along, Polly.'

The mare slashed downhill through the mist at a full gallop. The dog-cart leaped and bounded, until I thought we were all going to final smash together, and the dimly seen trees and hedgerows were past us with a wink and a dazzle. We rounded the corner at a more moderate pace and came into the straight highroad which leads from Brays Horton to Castle Barfield.

'We're close by now, sir,' I said, and the doctor drew down to a smart trot.

My mother had lined my ragged old jacket for me with coarse calico against the winter's cold, and I had thrown it down in such a posture that I could see it shining white against the murky darkness of the road.

'Here it is, sir.'

The doctor pulled up with a jerk, and leaped from the dog-cart. The policeman lifted me into the doctor's arms and I found the place where the two injured men lay, with the feet of one pointing to the head of the other. The officer had a bull's-eye lantern with him, and turned its light on Mr. Allardyce's face.

'My God!' he said. 'They've given him a doin'.'

'They have so,' said the doctor, stepping into the ditch beside him and snatching the lantern from the policeman's hand.

'Is he alive?' asked my father's voice, feebly.

'No credit to you if he is, Salter,' said the doctor, angrily. 'Here, Wilkins, give me a hand with him. A better fellow never broke bread,' he said later, when they had lifted the unconscious gentleman to the bank, and he was feeling hurriedly and softly about him. 'But he's as full of cranks as an old ship's biscuit 's full of weevils.'

‘He fowt well,’ said my father, in that difficult and painful voice, ‘but he got wuss mauled than I did.’

‘Look to that fellow, Wilkins,’ said the doctor. ‘See if you can get him on his legs.’

‘I think I could with a bit of help,’ said father; but when the officer tried to raise him he cried out sharply and bitterly, and the policeman, in his flurry, letting him fall, he gave so weak and yet so keen a groan that my heart stood still.

‘Oh, please, please, sir, see to father,’ I cried out.

‘Your father must take his turn, my lad,’ said the doctor gruffly but not unkindly. ‘I've only got one pair of hands.’

As to what means he took I can say nothing, but the policeman hurried away and beat up help, which came in the course of time, and the doctor's groom came down from Quarrymoor with a perfect procession behind him, and, at the end, gates were unshipped from their hinges, and Mr. Allardyce was carried one way, attended by the doctor and the crowd, and my father was borne another, whilst I followed, weeping, in his train.

CHAPTER VI

I HAD enough to cry for, if I had only known it, and even knowing what I did, I was sufficiently miserable. I was tired pretty nearly to death for one thing, and for another, I had been pretty smartly knocked on the head by one of the rascally gang which had almost killed father and Mr. Allardyce. I was too dazed and stupid and sore-headed to take everything in its full force, and in spite of the precocity which poverty forces, I was still little more than a baby.

My father lay on the unshipped gate, and the volunteers who had followed the doctor's man from Quarrymoor carried him along through the fog with a shuffling and uneasy step. Every now and then he gave a deep groan, which sounded awful in my ears; but in a while these sounds of suffering ceased, and then I began to be tormented by a still more dreadful fear. I think the party of bearers numbered seven. They relieved each other pretty often, and I trotted behind, sobbing and terror-stricken.

'Wheer's he to be took to?' one asked.

'The kid 'll tell us,' said another; and as well as my jerking throat and sobbing breath would let me do it, I directed them to our house.

There was the shifting fog, now hiding and now half revealing familiar objects. There was the well known smell of the brick-kilns, nauseous on the thick air. Here came the tinkle, tinkle, tinkle of the little hammers on the little anvils. There was never, I think, an hour in the twenty-four, week in, week out, Sundays or work-days, but that significant noise might be heard in some of the twenty-four cottages which made up our row.

‘This is the house,’ I said at last, and the men set down the gate on the road, and one of them, advancing to the door, knocked at it gently.

The unshuttered window was dark, but mother had evidently been sitting up in expectation of our return, and she answered the summons instantly.

‘Your man’s come to a bit of mischief, missis,’ said one of the bearers. ‘I’m afraid he’s hurt rather bad. Can you get us a bit of light to carry him in by?’

Mother never spoke a word in answer, but walked indoors as if the news had been the most commonplace in the world. I heard the splutter of a match, and then saw the growing light of a candle. She came back to the doorway, shading the rushlight with her hand, and peering into the darkness of the night. When her glance fell upon the figure of my father lying prone and helpless on the gate, I saw a curious twitch pass across her face, and she shivered as if with cold.

‘You’d best bring him in,’ she said; and when two or three of them stooped to take up their burden as before, she added: ‘There’ll be no room for that, lads.’

So two took him, one by the shoulders and one by the knees, and in that wise they carried him indoors, his body sagging in their hands as helpless as a sack.

They laid him down on the bed in the kitchen between the meagre fireplace and the window, and mother went down on her knees with the candle still in her hand, and looked at him.

I saw now that his face was very badly battered, and the caked blood from a wound on his forehead made him look worse than he really was.

‘What’s been done to him?’ my mother asked.

Her voice had not quite its natural tone, and her eyes looked strained and staring, but that was all.

‘Well,’ said one of the bearers, scratching his head, and looking down at her, vacantly, ‘I reckon he’s been knob-sticked, missis.’

‘Wheer was he?’ asked mother.

‘Mid-road twixt here an’ Parson’s Lane,’ said another of the men.

‘Well,’ said mother, rising from her knees and setting the old flat tin candle-stick on the table, ‘I must see to him, I reckon. Thank you for your trouble, lads. Thank ye kindly.’

They took this as an intimation that they might go, and went out lumbering one by one, awkwardly sympathetic, but not knowing how to express themselves, and so taking a wordless leave.

‘Jack,’ said mother, ‘take the kettle into ole Blowhard. He’s at work to-night, and you can hot up the water a bit on his fire. I’ve got none, as it happens.’

I don’t know how it came about, but I obeyed. I was perfectly aware of the truth. I knew as well then as I know now, that Blowhard had been one of my father’s assailants, and I would almost as soon I think, faced the devil, but I obeyed without question.

I carried the half-filled kettle out by the back way, threading a road with the blindfold surety of custom among the obstacles of our own home forge, and found myself in a second or two at the open door of Old Blowhard’s brewhouse. There he was, unwashed, and with a bristly rime of dirty gray upon his lips and cheek and chin, and with his iron-gray hair sticking out in disorderly spikes all about his head as usual. His ragged shirt-sleeves were rolled up above the elbow, and his lean arms, with their thick cordage of sinew, were bare. I stood in the open doorway almost afraid for my life, for I believed it was his hand which had dealt me that cruel blow two hours earlier, and Old Blowhard had suddenly grown to the dimensions of an armed terror.

I tried to speak, but could find neither voice nor courage, and it was only when a shaking sob seemed to explode within my breast that he looked up. He laid the iron rod at which he had been working and the hammer side by side on the anvil blade and stared at me.

‘Well,’ he asked, ‘what dost thee want?’

I managed to let him know my errand somehow, and he signed to me to enter.

‘What dost want hot water for at this time o’ night?’ he demanded.

‘Father’s been hurt,’ I said, ‘and mother wants the water for him.’

‘Hurt?’ he repeated, breathing hard and looking at me sideways, with an aspect of eager suspicion. ‘How hurt?’

He took the kettle from me as he spoke, and setting it on the hearth of the forge, raked the embers together with the toy shovel they all used at their work, and then took a mechanical pull at the bellows, still with that side-long glance at me.

'He's been knob-sticked,' I answered, repeating the phrase I had heard a few minutes earlier, but without any real knowledge of its meaning.

'Oh!' said Old Blowhard. 'He has, has he? **That's** nothin' to be wondered at.'

He gave a new rake among the embers which, under the first puff of the bellows, had begun to glow, and balancing the kettle on the brightest part of the fire, went on with his up and down mechanical motion of the hand, until the small fire glowed white hot, and the kettle began to sing. All the time he kept his side-long, wary glance on me, occasionally moistening his dry lips with his tongue.

'Who done it?' he asked at length.

I did not dare to answer for my soul.

'Who done it?' he repeated, still working at the bellows, though the kettle at this time was already boiling over, and a fierce column of steam, ruddy with the reflection of the fire, issued from the spout.

Still I gave him no answer, and he turned to lift the kettle from the fire, taking his ragged blackened apron of old sacking in his hand to do it. He set it on the floor at my feet, and his face being thus brought to about a level with my own, he stared me in the face.

'Was you theer?' he asked; and I made some sort of motion of the eyes, or gesture of the head, which he construed into a 'yes.' He knew whether I had been there well enough. 'Don't you let us have no fause charges about it,' he said, shaking a hand at me, still enveloped in the cover of the dirty sacking. 'Understand what I'm a-sayin' to thee. If theer's anny fause charges made, it's as like as not as them as knob-sticked thy feyther 'll knob-stick thee. Soak that in, my lad. A still tongue an' a wise yed. Soak it in. Theer's the kettle.'

Remembering the precaution he had used, I touched it gingerly, but finding that I could handle it without pain, I carried it away saying nothing, but horribly afraid of Old Blowhard, and desolate beyond expression.

My mother, when I got back, was kneeling by the side of the bed holding one of father's hands; but she had in the meantime, found somewhere a piece of soft white rag, and when I had brought her a little cold water in a tin cup, she raised that to a fitting temperature by an addition from the kettle, and began gently to clean father's face with it. I stood looking on quite helpless and forlorn. The lax posture of the figure on the bed, the amazing quietude with which my mother seemed to accept this extraordinary incident, my own fatigue and the blow I had received, all helped to make the matter on the surface seem as if it were a thing of no importance, although deeper down I know I tasted the misery and desolation of it as least as bitterly as a grown man might do.

The alternate dull roar and light tinkle of Old Blowhard's forge had ceased, and in the silence I heard a door open near at hand. It screeched slightly on the sanded brick floor, and then a step sounded in the street and came nearer. Our own front door had remained open, as the men who had borne my father home had left it, and the footsteps coming our way, paused there. Old Blowhard's wife stood in the doorway, and after an uncertain look of inquiry, she entered.

'Ourn tells me,' she said, 'as yourn's got into trouble.'

'It looks like it,' my mother answered stolidly, squeezing the blood-stained rag, and dipping in the battered tin cup for more water.

'If I could do anythin'——' said Blowhard's wife.

'Thank ye kindly,' said mother. 'Nothin' as far as I can see.'

Blowhard's wife took the candle in her hand and bent above the bed.

'Eh!' she said, with a soft, slow expulsion of the breath, as if the sight hurt her.

'You may well say that,' mother answered her.

'Poor lad!' said Blowhard's wife, 'they've served him cruel.'

'Yes,' said mother, with the same astonishing quiet she had shown from the first. 'They've served him cruel. He was the best among 'em, an' th' only one as tried to do a bit o' good to anybody. I've looked for it night an' day,' she went on; 'I'm none amazed.'

'Poor lad!' said Blowhard's wife. 'It's as pity he couldn't let things be.'

'Yes,' returned mother; 'that's what a many of 'em 'ud say when they crucified the Lord.'

The old woman stared rather stupidly at her, and I don't suppose that she had the faintest idea of the meaning of the words.

'Hast a notion,' she asked, 'who done it?'

'Jack was theer,' said mother. 'I've had no heart to ask him.'

At this, Old Blowhard's wife turned upon me, but I was so shaken with cowardice that I dared not speak a word of what I knew. Mr. Allardyce and father were walking together when half a dozen men or more, sprang out on them. There was a fight. I was knocked on the head and went to sleep. That, I remember, was my reading of the case. Then I woke, and found both badly hurt, and ran to Quarrymoor for the doctor.

'But was theer no word o' what was comin'?' Blowhard's wife asked me. 'The lad's young, but he's sharp,' she added to my mother. 'He'd know 'em in the dark onless they was all strangers.'

I began to quake exceedingly.

'Some on 'em spoke surely?' she pressed me.

'Yes,' I answered, 'some of them.'

'An' you didn't know 'em?' she asked; and I answering nothing, and daring to answer nothing, she added, 'They'd be strangers. Them as set 'em on 'ud see to that.'

'Yes,' said mother, as if she made the most commonplace statement in the world. 'Mr. Sim 'ud see to that.'

'Mary!' cried Blowhard's wife.

'He'd see to that,' said mother, either not noticing or else ignoring the warning cry. 'Sim's no fool, an' of course we shall never have a proof agen him.'

'You don't think——' said Blowhard's wife.

'I know,' said mother.

There was a lengthy silence after this, and my father was the first to break it. He opened his eyes and looked around with an absence of recognition of a place so familiar which was ghastly even to a child. But in a minute his look cleared and he knew where he was.

'Well, my pretty wench!' he said, and at that my mother sank down at the bedside where she had been kneeling, and began to cry with the blood-stained water-sodden rag at her eyes.

He stretched out a wandering hand to comfort her, but could not reach her, and on a sudden all the pent-up suffering and suspense I had known forced themselves to a relief and I ran outside to cry.

I don't know how time went, but I have some remembrance of Mrs. Blowhard shuffling from our house into her own, and of my mother coming out to coax me to lie down. I supposed that when I obeyed her I slept, but I have no certainty about it, and I only know that when I next remember anything the candle was still burning, mother was standing by the bed on one side, and on the other, sat the doctor in our only chair, with a watch in one hand and father's wrist in the other.

'H'm!' said the doctor, dropping the wrist and pocketing the watch. 'Mr. Allardyce seems to have got the worst of it.'

'He's pretty bad then?' said mother.

She spoke with the same strange quiet with which she had acted all along, but I could see by the red rims of her eyes and the stained pallor of her face that she had been crying since I had last looked at her.

'Yes,' the doctor answered, 'he's pretty bad, as you say. I'm not quite sure yet that it isn't a case of murder.'

He was calmly busy about his patient as he spoke, and he remained with us for I dare say half an hour, plastering and bandaging.

He had brought a small black bag with him, which seemed to hold everything he wanted, and at the finish he took a bottle from it, and gave my mother very particular directions as to what she should do with its contents.

'And now,' he said, struggling into his overcoat, and opening the door to look out on the fog, 'I'll make it my business to-morrow to send to the relieving officer. You'll have to send your man into the infirmary at the workhouse.'

'The Bastille!' cried my mother, clasping both hands together and regarding him with a look of terror.

'Well,' said the doctor coolly, 'he can't be properly nursed here, that's pretty evident.'

'Theer was never none o' mine in the Bastille!' cried my mother.

My good woman,' the doctor answered, 'you can't help yourself. You want your husband to live, I suppose? The workhouse infirmary is the proper place for him. He'll be well taken care of there, and if he's well taken care of, he'll pull through in all likelihood. If anybody were fool enough to keep him here, he'd die, to a dead certainty.' He added, tugging at a fur-lined glove: 'What must be must, you know, and if you only knew when you were well off you'd thank God there was such a place to go to.'

As a matter of fact, I suppose, the poor ought to be grateful for such help as they get at the hands of the Poor Law, but for some reason—not perhaps so very hard to find—the gaol itself is not more dreaded, and not even a sentence in the dock seems to inflict a deeper stigma or one that stings more.

'Now, don't you be silly about it,' said the doctor, seeing my mother quite broken by the shock of his intelligence. 'You want to save your man, don't you? Of course you do. And if that's the only way to do it, why—you must do it that way. He'll be thoroughly well taken care of. He'll get good food, good nursing, all sorts of proper comforts. What the devil is there in that to cry for? '

The query sounded unanswerable as he put it, but all the same my mother cried, and continued to cry, until I cried myself to sleep and forgot all about everything, as, thank Heaven, a tired child, however miserable, can.

But next day, when the doctor and the relieving officer turned up together, it was thought advisable to leave the patient where he was rather than run the risk of removing him.

'The poor beggar's so beastly low,' said the doctor. 'If he'd been properly nourished I should have better hope of him.'

'A good nourishing soup's the thing,' said the relieving officer.

'Properly made,' returned the doctor.

'I've got no authority, you know,' said the officer, who was an aged man with as kind a face as I ever saw in my life. 'If I was to take this kind o' thing up as often as I should like to—why, what about my income? '

'Just so,' said the doctor. 'What about mine if I did the same? '

'Exactly,' said the other—'exactly; that's wheer it is.'

'You must use your own discretion, of course,' said the doctor, buttoning himself into his coat, as if to say he resigned all further responsibility. 'The man's in the Barfield Union, and if he dies in your district, I'm not answerable for it. I've done what I can in a case of emergency, and I don't see how I can be expected to do any more.'

'Well,' said the officer, 'I'll assoom the responsibility, as far as half-a-crown goes. Look here, my woman. You've got a saucepan. Very well. A couple o' pound o' shin o' beef, lean an' fresh; two pints o' water; a pinch o' salt. Simmer slowly.'

'And a tablespoonful,' chimed in the doctor, 'as often as he'll take it.'

'*You've* got a pair o' legs on you,' said the relieving officer, turning on me, and looking mildly and benevolently at me from under a pair of bushy eyebrows. 'Run up into Barfield High Street and find the house o' Mr. Joseph Brambler.'

I said I knew it, and that Mr. Joseph Brambler was a friend of father's. I had heard my father say so, and was very proud of it.

'Tell him what's happened, and ask him to be so good as to let me know if I can see him to-night. Tek that envelope. It's got my name and address on it, To be so good as send word to me if I can see him to-night. You can remember that? '

Oh yes, I could remember that. I repeated it to show I was perfect in the lesson, and as I tied on my shabby little rag of a comforter, I heard the officer say that Mr. Joseph Brambler was the only chairman of guardians *he* had ever been able to get on with.

'He's got a heart for trouble,' said the aged man, 'whereas they're mostly that deadly afeard of the ratepayer.'

The doctor said, 'Damn the ratepayer! ' and the official answered that everybody knew where his own boot pinched him. All this was Greek to me at the time, but my mother having thrust a hunch of bread into my pocket, I set off upon my journey.

The fog had lifted, and but for the sense of trouble I had left behind me, the day would have smiled upon me. The small boy was at Mr. Brambler's gate as at my first visit, but he was used to me by this time, and though I found his airs and graces of superiority a little hard to bear, he was more easily sufferable than he had been.

I was passed into the house by the back way, and received by Mr. Jeremiah, who was as genially puzzled by the world as ever. He rattled coins in his pocket like Mr. Dick in 'Copperfield,' and having worn out this amusement in the course of some two or three minutes, took me by the shoulders and turned me round and round, chuckling meanwhile, as if he had a joke on hand.

'Come inside,' he said by-and-by. I'll show thee something.'

I followed, full of curiosity, for my fear of him had long since vanished, and he ushered me into that front-room, the first view of which had so overwhelmed my infant spirit. It was still glorious, but I could bear to look at it.

'That's summat like a chamber—eh? ' said Mr. Jeremiah; and when I responded 'Yes, sir,' he seemed, I thought, to miss something of my original fervour.

I can't tell how much is afterthought or later knowledge of obscure meaning, but I am writing honestly as well as I can remember.

'Look here,' he said, in what I thought a rather depressed fashion. 'Here's summat as you've never seen afore, I'll be bound.'

The something to which he drew my attention was a large, pot-bellied black case with a long thin neck, an affair like a legless and beheaded nigger. I suppose that the wonder and expectation in my look were satifactory for him, for he smiled with a beaming triumph. The mysterious case was just as mysterious to me as ever when he opened it, and showed, reposing in its inwards, a big 'cello. He took this out tenderly, and began to tune it, snapping at the cords with a forefinger, and letting his watery gray eyes wander all over the ceiling as he did so. By-and-by he got out his bow, and having plenteously resined it, he drew it across the strings, and produced a sonorous chord or two. Then he began to play, treating the instrument with pretty much the same stress and force with which he had banged the piano on the day on which I had first made acquaintance with him. His eyebrows were placed by nature in the middle of his forehead, instead of being just over his eyes, as most men's are; but in the course of playing they wandered up into his hair, and his facial grimace was not the least astonishing part of his performance.

From time to time he shot a glance of inquiry in my direction and on each occasion found me a prey to pure astonishment. This fact so gratified him, that it cost him the most terrible efforts not to smile. What I should think of his performance at this time of day, I cannot even guess, but I know very well that for surprise and interest it transcended everything I had until then seen or heard of in its way.

It went on for quite a quarter of an hour, and at the end of it, he so ran his fingers up and down the strings, and so made the instrument shriek and roar and moan, and so beat time with feet and head, that when he finished the perspiration stood in beads all over his face and forehead.

'Theer! ' he said, putting back the 'cello after carefully easing the strings. 'I'm a Don at that, anny way. That's a thing as I've allays been a Don at.' He laughed, and took his great stomach in both hands and hugged it in such a pride and self-gratulation as I have rarely seen; but cutting short this burst of mirth with a sudden solemnity, he bent down confidentially, and said: 'You ought to see my paintin's. That'—indicating the 'cello in its case—'that ain't the only thing as I'm a Don at. Come an' see my pictures.'

He was striding from the room, and I was in act to follow him, when the rattle of a latchkey sounded at the street door. He waved an urgent hand against me, and stood still, and as I shrank back in unconscious obedience to his gesture, Mr. Joseph entered.

He stared at both of us, and Mr. Jeremiah, waving an uncertain hand in my direction, murmured that here was 'that lad o' Salter's.'

'What he wants,' said Mr. Jeremiah feebly, 'I have not thought it my dooty to inquire into.'

Well,' asked Mr. Joseph crisply, 'and what does he want? '

I surrendered the addressed envelope which had been entrusted to me, and gave my message.

At the beginning of my story he stood with his feet apart and his hands rammed into his side-pockets, but before he had half heard me out he sat down abruptly, throwing his hat upon the table, and staring hard at me with knitted eyebrows. He breathed hard on an exclamation once or twice, and when I had brought my narrative to a close he rumpled his silvery hair with both hands.

'Theer, theer! ' he said, 'cryin' won't mend it. Come, come! That's a shillin'. Look at it. A brand new un, fresh from the mint. Jane! ' he walked out into the hall to shout for the servant. 'Jane! Oh, theer you are. Tek this child into the kitchen, and stretch his wescut for him. Then bring him back to me.'

I marched off in rear of Jane, and, troubled as I was in mind, and sore in body, I was still willing to have my waistcoat stretched, and submitted myself to Jane's ministrations with complete alacrity. Whilst I sat at the kitchen table I could hear Mr. Brambler moving and talking about in the yard, and made out that he was ordering the tax-cart to be got ready. When I had finished my meal the vehicle was standing in High Street. Mr. Brambler pitchforked me into it with small ceremony, and, mounting after me, took the reins and drove away without a word of explanation.

CHAPTER VII

HE drove straight to our house, and, having himself dismounted, helped me to the ground and went indoors, leaving the horse and cart unguarded. He nodded courtly at my mother, who bobbed a rustic salute at him, and walking to the side of the wretched bed, he looked down in silence for a full minute, or even more. Then he turned and closed the door.

'You're Mrs. Salter?' he asked.

'Yes,' said mother.

'My name's Brambler,' he told her, 'Mr. Joseph Brambler. You've heard your husband speak o' me.'

'Often and often,' she said.

'This is a black business,' said Mr. Brambler, 'and I'm bent at getting at the bottom on it. I suppose you've got some kind of a notion as to whose hand is in it.'

'I'm pretty sure, sir, for my own part,' mother answered.

'Least said, soonest mended,' said Mr. Brambler, 'but I've got my notions too. It's safest to name no names in a case like this till we can prove somethin', but may I ask if your ideas pints anywheer in the direction of Quarrymoor?'

'You never spoke a truer word than that, sir,' mother answered.

Mr. Brambler nodded with an exaggerated air of sagacity.

'Theer's a person livin' in that direction, ma'am,' he said, 'as has had the cheek and impertinence to put himself up agen me for a many years. I made that person, ma'am, in the mistaken kindness o' my heart. Now I'm goin' for him, an' if theer's justice in the land we'll have it. We'll have it, ma'am, if it costs me a hundred pound.

I'm good for more than that if needs be; but we'll have it, cost what it may.'

My mother was sure she thanked him, and thanked him from her heart.

'Nothin' to thank me for, ma'am,' said Mr. Brambler.

'I know full well,' said mother, 'theer's few o' the gentry as would dream of takin' trouble for poor folk as we be. But as for that theer Sim——'

'I beg your pardon, ma'am,' said Mr. Brambler. 'I'm a trifle hard of hearing at times. I didn't quite catch what you said, and, if *you* please'—holding up an imperative finger as she was about to speak it—'I'd rather not catch it. I expressed my opinion of a person livin' in the direction o' Quarrymoor, some ten or twelve 'ears back, and it cost me a trifle of three hundred pound. Now, whether that was the same person as I have in my eye this minute, or whether it wasn't the same person, meks no difference. I'm for being on the safe side. You can do as you like when I'm away, but my rule is to keep my teeth to guard my tongue and to refuse to listen to anny scandal about annybody.'

'It's the best way, I'm sure, sir,' mother answered.

'Now, mind ye,' said Mr. Brambler, seating himself in the one chair and spreading his hands upon his knees, 'I'm your friend in this matter. Your husband shan't be allowed to want for nothing so long as he's in this condition.'

'Oh, God bless you, sir!' said mother, and began to wipe her eyes with her apron.

'Hush your chatter, woman,' said Mr. Brambler severely, 'and let a man get a word in edgeways, will ye?'

'You shall have *my* thanks an' prayers as long as I live!' cried mother.

'Save 'em to cool your porridge,' said Mr. Brambler, 'an' let me speak. I've got my knife into a certain party, and I mean to keep it theer. I mean to twist it about a bit, an' this is one o' my ways o' doin' it: It belongs to the rights of ivery honest and hup-right man to abhor from a scoundrel. I abhor from that un, and I'm goin' to let him find it out. And now, to begin with, what's known about the rights an' wrongs o' this here affair? Has your man a notion of who set about him?'

‘ He’s hardly spoke a word since here he’s been,’ said mother.

‘ He’s hardly like to say much for one while, judging from the looks on him,’ said Mr. Brambler, after a new examination of my father’s face.

The bandaged head lay in the full mild autumn light which came in through the uncurtained window, and the features. where the bandages with their blood-stained edges left them visible, looked ghastly enough in all conscience. I can remember the bruised and battered face now as clearly as if I had it before me at this instant.

‘ Now, as for Mr. Allardyce,’ pursued Mr. Brambler, ‘ can he be talked to? ’

‘ The neighbours have been in this mornin’,’ mother told him, ‘ an’ they say he’s wuss served than ourn.’

‘ Well,’ said Mr. Brambler, ‘ we must tek what we can get. Here’s the lad. He was theer. What’s he got to say about it? ’

He began to question me, and thus delayed the statement I should have been ready to make. I am not very much ashamed of the confession I have already offered. I was a child. I had only newly entered my eight year. I was very much afraid of Blowhard and of Mr. Sim, and I had held my tongue through cowardice so far. Now that we had so powerful a person behind us as I supposed Mr. Brambler to be, my fears had more than half vanished from my mind, and I was willing to tell my story. But whilst he questioned me, and made himself very unlike himself in ponderous assumption of judicial faculty, and badgered me in pursuit of unnecessary detail, the door opened and old Blowhard’s wife came in with something under her apron. The something turned out to be a pot of tea, which the poor neighbourly creature had brought as a comfort for my mother.

‘ If I’m in the road—— ’ she said humbly, and was preparing to back out the house, when Mr. Brambler arrested her. I can only suppose that he was willing to be seen in his judicial form. He may not often have had a chance of appearing as the god out of the machine in a case which might result in a double charge of murder, and may have been disposed to make the most of that which presented itself. Perhaps I wrong the good old fellow, but I can find no other reason for his having kept Mrs. Blowhard as he did.

‘ This is a very dark an’ dirty business, ma’am,’ he said, ‘ an’ we're doin' our best, an' we mean to do our best, to get down to the rights an' wrongs on it.'

'It's a wicked thing, sir,' said Blowhard's wife.

'Now,' said Mr. Brambler, 'it's not for you to clack about it. I'm examinin' an important witness, a b'y as was present on the occasion referred to. Now, John Salter, junior, attend to me. On the night of Sunday, last past, last night, in fact, you was midway betwixt this an' Parsons Lane, which leads to Quarrymoor. You was in the company of your father and the Reverend Mr. Allardyce. Is them the facts?'

'Yes, sir.'

'You was all three sprung out upon by a number of men—it might ha' been four and it might ha' been six, but less than four an' more than six it was not. Is that right?'

'Yes, sir.'

If you was to stand on your own personal opinion, which, being but a child and startled, and knocked on the 'ed pretty early, is more than you feel inclined to do, you might say there was five of 'em. Is that the case?'

'Yes, sir.'

This was the barrister fashion in which he had treated me from the first, but I observed that even so small an addition to his public as Old Blowhard's wife made, inflated his sense of the importance of the inquiry and of his own position in it. Is it ungrateful, I wonder, to have these exasperating recollections of a man so good and kind and simple? I hope not. There is no sense of ingratitude in my heart and Mr. Joseph Brambler is not the only man I have known who has upon occasion obscured the virtues of a rare good heart by a veneer of vanity.

'Now,' said Mr. Brambler, leaning back in his chair and folding his arms to make himself the more judicially impressive, 'we'd got as fur as to understand from the witness as it was dark an' a bit foggy. You was understood to say as it was dark an' a bit foggy?'

'Yes, sir.'

'An', bein' dark an' a bit foggy, you did not by sight recognise any of the prisoners. That is to say,' he added, correcting himself, 'of them as will be the prisoners in doo time.'

'No, sir.'

'What do you mean by "No, sir"?' he queried severely.

'I couldn't tell 'em by sight,' I answered.

'Very well then,' he returned, unbending, 'men are to be known by their v'ices. Was any words exchanged betwixt the attackin' party an' your father, or Mr. Allardyce, or you?'

He looked around as if he approved of this way of doing business, and I thought I saw a touch of Brother Jeremiah in him. There was a facial resemblance—a family look which I had never observed before.

They were on us very quickly, I had to tell him, and nothing was said at the very first by our assailants. But I had heard voices, and I thought that I should know two of them if I heard them again. The last statement was made in answer to a direct question.

'Now, attend,' said Mr. Brambler. 'Here's the pint. Had you ever to your knowledge, heard any one o' them vi'ces before?'

Now, if it had not been for the presence of Blowhard's wife, I should have told the truth at once; but when this question came point-blank, I looked at her. Her soiled hand was at her lips, and both her hand and her lips were trembling. She was staring at me with a dreadful beseeching in her look, though I construed it at the time into something of a menace. But menace or beseeching, it was all the same to me, and so far as Old Blowhard was concerned, it sealed my lips. I could not name him in her presence, and I cannot tell whether it was fear or pity which kept me silent.

'Had you ever,' repeated Mr. Brambler, 'to your knowledge, heard any one of them v'ices before?'

'Yes,' I answered; and the trembling lips of Old Blowhard's wife were for one mere instant forsaken by the shaking hand.

'Oh,' said Mr. Brambler. 'Now we're gettin' to business, ma'am. You had, had you? When and wheer?'

'The same day,' I answered.

I suppose I should have answered 'yesterday' under ordinary conditions, but it looked as if the event about which I was being questioned had gone back a year or thereabouts.

'And wheer?' asked Mr. Brambler.

I related the story of the meeting in the field beyond Brays Horton, but I kept Blowhard's name out of it. I could see the terror fading out of the woman's face, but what I was saying still had an evident fascination for her, and she never took her glance away from me for a second.

'And what makes you so sure about the man?' Mr. Brambler asked me.

I answered that he 'talked funny.'

'Talked funny?' he echoed. 'How funny?'

I imitated him to the best of my ability, and I suppose not badly, for my questioner nodded and said: 'Ay, ay!' with obvious understanding.

'There can't be many on 'em like that. The man's got no roof to his mouth. He should be lighted upon pretty easy. An' now, my lad, give us what they said as near as you can remember.'

I repeated the talk I had overheard, but with that woman's eyes on me I had to leave Old Blowhard out of the story, and so boggled, and became uncertain and unconvincing. But when I came to the statement that one of the men mistrusted Mr. Sim, and wouldn't do anything until he saw the colour of his money, because he had no spite against the man, Mr. Brambler suddenly clutched me by the arm.

'Who taught you to say them words?' he asked.

'Nobody taught me, sir,' I responded, shrinking back from him because he hurt me, and half frightened me into the bargain.

Did I know the nature of a hoath? he asked. No, I didn't. Did I know that if I told lies I should go to the naughty place? So much I knew. It was one of the cardinal points of my theology. Would I say 'Hangy bangy, cut my throat, and I hoped a lie would stick in my throat?' I would and did repeat this idiot formula with perfect sincerity.

'Very well,' said Mr. Brambler, rising. 'That'll do. What you've all got to understand is this: Not a word is to be spoken about this business by any one on us. When I get my knife into a man, I keep my knife in him, no matter whether he lives at Quarrymoor or Castle Barfield. Maybe I've got my knife into this wicked scoundrel as had a hand in this wicked affair.' He pointed to the bed. 'Maybe I haven't. Never mind; time'll show.'

With this, he made a grope in his breeches pockets with both hands, and brought out more money than I had ever seen in all my life before. If I had ever until then seen a gold coin I cannot tell, though I should be inclined to think it extremely improbable, but a dozen sovereigns sparkled in his open hands amongst a little mass of silver pieces, and I was as certain of their exceeding value as I should have been a dozen years later, when I had begun to be more familiar with their use and aspect.

A mad idea, to the effect that Mr. Brambler was going to make us all wealthy for life by the donation of this astounding heap of treasure, had scarcely had time to leap into my mind when he restored both fists to his pockets.

'No,' he said; 'better than money! I'll tell thee what I'll do missis. I'll send thee my own doctor—no parish games here! He shall leave written word as to what thy man's to have, an' be it what it may— heggs, soup, beef-tay, port wine, chicken—he shall have it as good as it can be got, and you can send up the little chap ivery day to see what's wanted. Now, now! Hush your noise. I can't abide a woman's cackle, and I niver could, an' that's why I've abode to be a bachelor.'

'God bless thee, master!' said Old Blowhard's wife. But he turned upon her with great fierceness, and asked her what the devil it had to do with her, and so went away, blowing his nose noisily, and, climbing into his tax-cart, he whipped up the patient horse, and drove headlong in the direction of Quarrymoor.

He pulled up before he had gone fifty yards, and turning the horse's head the other way, he passed our house at a plunging canter.

My mother had stood like one dazed at his sudden departure and the unlooked-for relief of the promise he had made, but he had scarce gone by when she fell upon her knees on the floor, and clipped me in her arms and kissed me.

'God's raised up a friend for us, Johnny!' she said brokenly. 'His name be praised!'

'Amen!' said Mrs. Blowhard. 'He's a good un if theer iver was.'

We all had a cry together, and Old Blowhard's wife poured out the tea she had brought. It was very black and pungent, and was sweetened with treacle, which came cheaper, I fancy, than even the commonest kind of sugar. They left me with a portion of it in a cracked saucer, and I had instructions to watch father whilst they went into the brewhouse, so that their talk might not disturb him.

There is a sense in which every thing is strange to an observant child, and there is a sense in which nothing is strange. I began to notice something odd in the demeanour of Old Blowhard's wife. She and my mother, I should tell you, had never been intimate associates. Poor as we were, and as we were likely to be, there was a recognised difference between ourselves and our neighbours. My father's children went to school—a phenomenal thing to begin with. We were shabby of course, but we were as clean as a general thing—at least we were as clean once a day as yellow soap and cold water and a coarse jack-towel—which served the whole household for at least a week—could make us. This was a circumstance which, in our row of cottages, was even more phenomenal than the schooling. Then, father was a man of astonishing erudition, and my poor mother had been better off and it was known that she might have married to high advantage. All these facts were recognised, and sometimes I carried a black eye or so because of them.

Old Blowhard and his family were at the other end of the social scale. When all were ignorant, and poor, and dirty, and ragged, and beery, when Heaven sent the chance of beer, Old Blowhard and his wife were the most ignorant, the poorest, dirtiest, raggedest and beeriest. We Salters, in point of fact, were the cultured aristocrats of that wretched community, and the Blowhards were at the other extreme. I don't think it ever enters the heads of people who have not had a familiar knowledge of the very poor, that there are any recognised social grades amongst them. But, as a matter of fact, the grades of society are simply infinite, and they are as definitely known and as unquestionably accepted there as they are between the inhabitants of Park Lane and the nobility and gentry of the Borough Road.

I certainly was not surprised that Old Blowhard's wife should be neighbourly in a time of trouble like our own, for that was a characteristic of the row, and if I had the time, or if this was the place for it, I could tell a hundred stories of kindness and self-sacrifice. But, from the moment at which she found me under Mr. Joseph Brambler's examination in my mother's kitchen, I saw that I was a subject of constant preoccupation and interest to Blowhard's wife.

The whole twenty-four cottages which made up the row had one long brick-paved back-yard in common, and beyond that lay the field, with no intervening hedge, ditch or wall.

Go when I would for the next two or three days into that back-yard, or venture when I would into the street, my whereabouts seemed to be known by some curious sympathetic process to Blowhard's wife, and she was out of doors to watch me.

My daily journeys to Mr. Brambler's house, laden with an empty basket on my walk to Barfield and with a full one on my home, brought me a plentiful regular meal, and when Blowhard's wife took to tempting me to her door with crusts and onions and cold potatoes, I was less eager to accept her invitation than I should have under customary conditions.

During all the time of my father's confinement to bed it fairly snowed meat and drink in our house. Beef-teas and soups, and calf's-foot jellies and cold chickens and extracts and potted things unheard of—cream and eggs and fresh butter, brandy and port wine, and I know not how many other strengthening and enticing delicacies were stowed away in the basket I carried. There was not only enough for the one invalid, who would have been a staunch trencherman indeed if he had consumed them all; but when his last wish and want was satisfied, there was enough for mother and the three hungry little mouths that opened around her; and Mr. Brambler's charity overflowed on the neighbours, and Blowhard's little girl, being down with a low fever, familiar to the region (for which the stench of the brick-kilns and a low diet were mainly responsible), was helped to life and strength from these liberal stores. We had never been so well off in our lives, I may safely say, and for many a year thereafter were never so well off again as we were under Mr. Joseph Brambler's enthusiastic patronage.

It happened one afternoon when I was sent to Mr. Brambler's house, and came back with an unusual load, that I was deputed by my mother to carry into Blowhard's house a teacupful of calf's-foot jelly and an orange for the solace of Blowhard's girl.

The old woman was absent, and when I tapped at the back-door I heard the accustomed wheeze of the bellows and the accustomed hum of the little fire, and Old Blowhard was singing some sort of tuneless song in time to the clink of the hammer on the anvil.

The man had lost none of the terrors he had recently acquired to me, and I was more than half afraid to enter, but when I had rapped a second or third time, he called out to me to come in and be damned to me.

I obeyed his command with trembling, and pushing open the unlatched door with my shoulder, stood there with the cup in one hand and the orange in the other.

'If you please,' I said.

Old Blowhard suspended his hammering, and looking very hard at me, began to comb his hair with the handle of the little hammer.

He scowled so that he fairly frightened me, and whilst he stared, he swallowed two or three times, nodding each time across the anvil, as if he were theatening to swallow me.

'How's the feyther?' he asked at last in a gruff voice.

'He's better,' I answered; 'he's able to sit up in bed.'

'Ah!' said Blowhard, 'what ha' you got theer?'

'If you please,' I said, 'mother thinks these might be good for Lucy.'

Blowhard went again through that swallowing motion, jerking out his bristly chin each time.

'Come in,' he said. 'Set 'em down.'

I set the cup and orange on the wooden foundation of the tiny anvil the child had been used to work at, and would have fain gone away again, but the man detained me.

'Look here,' he said, with a laboured slowness, 'is your feyther sensible?'

'Yes,' I answered.

'Does he know as you're bringin' them things in here?'

'Yes.'

He combed his hair with the handle of the hammer, and scratched it into disorder again with his unengaged hand.

'Has he got any sort of a idea,' he began, and then paused so long that I made once more a motion towards the doorway.

He moved forward and hooked me back with the head of the hammer.

'Look here, Johnny. Does he know who done that?'

I knew so unfailingly what he meant to express, and I was so certain of his own guilt, and so afraid of him, that I could do nothing but pant in an agonized silence.

‘D’ye hear? ’ he asked, but I stared at him in a petrified inability to answer.

‘I’m beholden,’ he said, beating on the little anvil with the little hammer to emphasize his speech, ‘to no man. Least of all I’m beholden to Jack Salter. Tek them things away, an’ niver let me see thy ugly young mug again.’

He came round the anvil and I retired before him, and the door still remaining open, I backed into the yard.

He took up the cup and the orange and hurled them away into the frouzy field which lay at the back of the row.

‘Now,’ he said, ‘gerrout! or I’ll send thee after ’em.’

As I recoiled from him, in fear of his threatening voice and hand, my mother spoke. She was standing at the back door of our cottage wringing out some sort of a rough cloth in both hands.

‘That’s a neighbourlike sort of a thing, Blowhard,’ she said. ‘Good stuff o’ that kind’s none so plenty hereabouts as you can afford to play with it.’

‘Who gi’en you the right,’ cried Blowhard, with a grisly expletive —‘who gi’en you the right to offer charity to me or mine? Did I iver ax for charity? ’

‘There’s a many,’ said my mother, ‘as niver need to ask for charity, so long as they’re content to tek the wage for crime.’

Blowhard went pale under the unwashed grime of years, and fell back on his own door-jamb.

‘Come in, Jack,’ said mother; and I followed her indoors, wondering how she knew, for I had never dared to breathe a word.

CHAPTER VIII

FATHER was better by this time, and spent a good part of the day propped up in bed. He was still ghastly with bandages, and his eyes had sunk far back into his head, and had grown preternaturally large so that at times I was more than half afraid of him. When mother and I got back into the kitchen he held one of his favourite books, in both hands, but he was too weak to read it, and had suffered it to fall on the counterpane. He looked up with a faint distorted smile as we entered, and mother, wiping her hands on her coarse apron, sat down and began to work at some bit of mending she had begun the day before.

'Well, my lass,' said father, after a longish spell of quiet, 'what is it?'

There was this notable thing about my parents—that each seemed to read the other like an open page. Any mood in the least out of the common in the mind of either was detected instantly by the other. Of course I have seen something of this in many other cases, but I have never known it in the same degree. With them, it seemed to be a sort of unfailing instinct.

'Naught, lad, naught!' said mother, sewing away industriously.

'Come, my lass,' said father, 'what is it?'

His voice was very weak and husky, and I thought my mother's answer very natural.

'Jack, my lad,' she said, 'I'm none for fretting a sick man wi' a silly woman's fancies. Thee lie still and get mended.'

'It's no way for me to mend to see thee fretted,' father answered.

'I'm none fretted,' said mother.

'That thou art,' he said, 'and hast rayson, I'll be bound. Run and play yourself awhile, Jack.'

'Nay,' said mother, 'there's no need to drive the child away. I've had a bit of a turn-up with Ode Blowhard. I sent a bit o' comfort round for his missis, and he chucked it out o' doors. That's all. I gi'en him a bit o' my mind, but there's nothin' to be upset about.'

'Chucked it out o' doors, did he?' said father in a thoughtful way. 'Ah!'

'You may as well say that!' cried mother, biting off a thread as she spoke, and looking keenly at him sideways.

'Why, how now?' said father, turning his pale face and sunken eyes upon her.

'A nod's as good as a wink to a blind horse,' said mother.

She tried hard for a customary tone, but her voice trembled and her hands shook so that her attempt to thread her needle resulted in sheer failure.

Father looked at her with a half-troubled, half-wondering glance but she avoided his eyes elaborately, and by-and-by he relaxed his attitude and suffered his head, which he had only half-raised from the pillow, to fall back again.

'I'm a bit too tired to spend my time on riddles,' he said, and so closed his eyes, and in a little while seemed to have fallen off to sleep.

In the course of the next quarter of an hour mother often looked in his direction, and at last, being satisfied that he slept, she got up cautiously from the chair, and slipping quietly to the workshop, beckoned me to follow.

I obeyed, making as little noise as I could, and when we were once out of the front room, mother essayed to close the door; but the crazy boards of which it was made, and its creaking hinges, and the scratching noise of its hanging timbers on the gritted floor, warned her almost at the first movement, and she desisted. She led me to the far corner of the room where ever since I could remember, until quite lately, the bellows had wheezed, and the little fire of slack and coke had alternately roared and slumbered.

'Johnny,' she began, in an impressive whisper, bending over me, and laying her toil-hardened hand upon my shoulder, 'you'll tell your mother the truth. Now, won't you?'

I said, ' Yes.' I knew as well as possible what was coming, but since she had defied Old Blowhard, and had frightened him so by her defiance, I was no longer afraid.

' The night they set about father,' she said, still whispering, and looking, not at me, but over my head at the door between us and the room where father was asleep, ' Blowhard was among 'em? '

' Yes,' I said; ' I heard him speak.'

' That'll do,' she answered, and leaving me there, she went back to her seat and took up her sewing.

I had many a time upbraided myself, child as I was, for my cowardly silence, but never so much as then, when she forbore to ask me a word about my reasons for it. We talked often about the matter afterwards when I had grown older, and I know then that she understood me and forgave me then. I had a good cry about it in the lonely fields that afternoon, and raged with transports of childish vengeance against Blowhard.

I remember a vision of extreme solace, in which the solitary policeman of Quarrymoor marched Blowhard into captivity, and I so clearly saw him hanged that the fancy is like a picture in my mind this moment: Blowhard in his working dress, looking exactly as I had always known him, with a rope round his neck, and his feet off the ground, and his eyes wide open, threatening me. This fancy was so far from bringing solace that I ran home to be out of the way of it, but it got into a knack of coming back at night-time, and for a week or two, until other events killed it, made the old rascal a sleeping as well as walking dread to me.

I was pretty often despatched to Quarrymoor in those days, to ask for news of Mr. Allardyce. He seemed at first to have been more damaged than my father, but he was the first to begin to gather strength. He had no more willing nursing, but I dare say his treatment was the more skilful, and apart from that he had youth on his side, and had never had to submit to the lifelong privations which must have weakened my father's constitution.

The news I was able to bring back about him grew more and more and more reassuring, and at last when I called I was ordered into his presence.

I found him seated near the window in the room in which father had once taken tea with him. He had always been lank and thin, but now, after long suffering and confinement to his room, he looked half transparent, and only half substantial. He had no sign of injury about the head or face, as my father still had, and in some vague or undetermined manner that fact seemed in my mind to be associated with the other fact that Mr. Allardyce was a gentleman. I am quite sure that I had not expected to find him disfigured, and that if I had done so it would have been a good deal of a shock to me. He received me kindly, and made me sit down whilst he talked to me.

'Well, Johnnie,' he began, 'what is the news about your father?'

I told him how kindly and generously Mr. Brambler had behaved, and how well cared for we had been since he had heard of father's misfortune. I could see that he was pleased at this, for he nodded smilingly from time to time. I dare say I put a splendid unconscious relish into my mention of the various delicacies with which we were kept supplied.

'Soup *an'* biled chicken, *an'* fresh eggs, *an'* tea, *an'* wined *an'* oranges, *an'* nuts.'

'No, no, Johnnie,' he interrupted me, 'not nuts, I think.'

I am afraid the nuts were a mere matter of youthful fervour, and I hung my head awhile.

'Now, tell me. Has your father any idea who set on him that night?'

'I don't know, sir, if father has,' I answered; 'mother has.'

I suppose he thought me too young to be questioned on a matter of such moment, for though I was burning to tell him more about Old Blowhard, he asked no more, but simply nodded to indicate that he had heard me.

He made the housekeeper bring me a thick slice of bread and jam, which she did with rather an evil grace, I thought, and whilst I nervously despatched it, made casual inquiries about my lessons, and finally dismissed me with a sixpence, and the news that he was to be allowed to drive out on the morrow, and would pass our cottage about mid-day.

'I shall not be able to come in,' he said, 'for the doctor has ordered me to make no calls, but I will stop there for a moment, and perhaps your mother will come out to speak to me.'

I was sure she would be glad to see him about again, and in my clumsy way, I said so.

'Very well,' he said. 'Shake hands, little man, and run away home.'

He sank back wearily in his chair as I left him, and I ran back the whole of the way as fast as my legs would carry me to bear the joyful news.

My father was elated by it, for, mother excepted, he had no such respect and affection for any living creature as he had for Mr. Allardyce. He was positively out of bed next day, and when at noontide, according to promise, the curate was driven up to the door in an open fly, he managed to get out into the street to meet him, leaning on mother's arm.

Mr. Allardyce shook hands with him, the whole row looking on from the front doors. Old Blowhard was there, scowling, and blinking in the sunlight like an owl, swinging a hammer in one hand and with the other ruffling his disordered grizzly hair.

Mr. Allardyce saw him, and hailed him in his clear weak voice, using the only name he knew him by.

'Good morning, Blowhard.'

It was the Black Country habit in my early days so to sink a man's identity under a nickname that his real name was often forgotten. I have actually known cases where men have married under a nickname bestowed upon their fathers, without the remotest idea that they were parting with anything which belonged to them.

Blowhard for sole answer bolted into his house.

'What's the matter with that fellow, eh, Salter?' asked Mr. Allardyce.

'Never mind him, sir,' said father. 'He's a knotted bit o' stuff is Blowhard. The sight o' you's good for sore eyes, sir.'

Poor old father was still ghastly with his bandages, and Mr. Allardyce looked at him piteously.

'They seem to have mauled you pretty badly, Salter,' he said.

'Why, yes, sir,' father answered, as if it were a rather commonplace concern.

'They came for you, of course,' said the parson. 'I got my share simply because I happened to be with you.'

He put that half questioningly, and my father answered that he supposed it happened so.

My mother broke in there, with a voice of authority, and put an end to the colloquy.

'All respects to you, but this is quite enough for Salter.'

'I am sure it must be,' said Mr. Allardyce. 'Good-bye, Salter; good-bye, Mrs. Salter. I shall be driving by every day for a time, and I'll look in to see how you are getting on.'

With that he shook hands with father and drove away, and we all went back into the cottage.

Father was so weak and tired that he had to be helped on to the bed, where he fell asleep in almost no time.

Mother rated him in a grumbling undertone for his foolhardiness in rising and dressing at all, and even after his closed eyes and even breathing told us that he was fast asleep, she girded at him; but when she had finished she sat quiet for a time over her mending, and then she said, as I remember her saying a hundred times:

'Niver you forget your father, Johnnie. He's a man to be proud on. I've met a lot o' people i' *my* day, and I've niver sin his like, an' niver look to.'

The good tender soul! Her bark was always a sheep dog's warning, and she never worried a member of her flock.

Mr. Allardyce came again, and yet again, and day by day he came, and every day my father, growing stronger and stronger, went out to meet him, until at last they came into the house together.

Now, you must understand that in all her married life, at least since the time when her first child was born, my mother had found no chance of showing how clean and neat and tidy and contriving a housewife she could be. But, thanks to Mr. Allardyce's loyalty to father, and thanks to Mr. Joseph Brambler's lusty hate of Mr. Sim, and his championship of father's cause, we were better off than we had ever been in our lives, and for weeks now my mother's whole duty had been to nurse father and to make the household comfortable and bright, so far as our means would go.

I don't suppose that such a thing was ever seen in a nailer's cottage before or since our day, but there was a clean bit of cheap crinkled white muslin in the front window, and behind it on the shelf, were two geranium pots. All the poor shabby place was scrubbed and scoured and darned and mended, until, though I had seen the glories of Mr. Brambler's house, I was proud that a gentleman should walk into ours.

We had three chairs now; for Mr. Joseph Brambler, calling one day and finding us provided with but one, had sent two second-hand cheap wooden articles in a hand-cart that very afternoon. I thought the renovated place a palace, and I think now, very tenderly and sadly, of my mother's modest pride in it.

What a hard and bitter life it was to be sure, and yet what simple compensations there were in it!

Mr. Allardyce shook hands with father warmly, as he always did when they met, and came indoors, leaving the hired open fly to be stared at by the inhabitants of the row, to my intense pride and gratification.

This special visit from Mr. Allardyce turned out to be a very solemn occasion. He and father and mother sat in conclave to decide what was to be done in respect to the murderous assault of now nearly seven weeks ago. Facts came out of which I had known nothing. Blowhard and the rest of his gang had all been noticeable, so it appeared, from the fact that they had been spending in drink a great deal more money than they could have come by honestly in the course of labour, even if they had left their families to starve and had devoted the whole proceeds of work to their orgies. The fact that their riches had not been come by through work was made still clearer by the other fact that they had hardly been working at all for a week or two after the event. They were clumsy and ignorant and unwary in the extreme, for they had been seen together before the assault and since, and the common suspicions pointed at them. Mr. Allardyce had recognised one fellow—a parishioner of his own—by his voice. Father was sure of two others, and now the question was as to what should be done. Mother was all for handing them over to the police at once, and I think father was of the same opinion; but they both reckoned without Mr. Allardyce, who was a kind of Christian Quixote.

I can't say, and I dare not say, that he did anything but follow the creed of the Master whom he preached, but he was in favour of forgiving all this scum, and melting their hearts in that way. That problem is a very big one, and if the greatest and most wonderful Leader the world has ever known decided it in one way nearly two thousand years ago, it is perfectly certain that the world at large has gone on deciding it ever since in a totally different fashion.

'But,' said Mr. Allardyce, 'what is the good of our pretending to be followers of Christ if, with His words on our lips, we walk deliberately away from Him? Why is it our daily and hourly prayer to be delivered from human angers and revenges, if at the first temptation we give way to them?'

I am not sure that any such daily and hourly prayer was offered up in our house by anybody. We were only a decent, law-abiding family, and knew very little about those spiritual fervours which animated Mr. Allardyce.

If the Reverend Tommy had visited us with such a doctrine he would have been laughed to scorn; but his curate was a person of a very different type. His cultured and gentle voice, his mild and persuasive eye, the soft eloquence of his manner, and, most of all, the fact that he was father's benefactor and fellow-sufferer, gave his arguments a force which could not have belonged to those of any other man, and in the end he conquered.

'These poor fellows,' said Mr. Allardyce, 'must know that they are detected, and that we have it in our power to punish them; without that we can teach them no lesson. We will begin with Blowhard. John, run round to Mr. Blowhard's cottage and say that your father and I desire to see him.'

I undertook this message with no great willingness, but its execution was made simple for me.

Blowhard was at his own door in conference with a neighbour, and both he and the neighbour were staring at the open fly which still stood in front of our house.

'Blowhard,' said I, speaking from a safe distance, 'you'm wanted.'

'Wanted, be I?' said Blowhard. 'Wheer?'

'Mr. Allardyce wants you,' I returned.

'Does he?' asked Blowhard, with a short, explosive laugh of one syllable. 'Let him want, and be —— to him.'

This brief colloquy was perfectly audible within doors, and before I had quite decided to return without a further effort, Mr. Allardyce walked into the street. He had entered our house quite weak and tottering, but he walked towards old Blowhard erect and like a man in full health.

The blackguard looked at him as he approached, and I read in his half-scared, half-lowering eye that he was divided in his mind between attack and retreat .

'Come with me,' said Mr. Allardyce very quietly. 'I have something to say to you.'

'Say it,' said Blowhard, wheezing noisily, and turning gray under his grime.

'Shall I say it?' asked Mr. Allardyce. 'Here? Do you really wish me to say it here?'

'Say it wheer you like,' said Blowhard.

'If I say it here,' returned Mr. Allardyce, cool and calm, 'I shall certainly have to say it elsewhere. Now, for your sake, I don't want to do that. Come!'

He took Blowhard's dirty shirt-sleeve between his thumb and finger, and the man came with him more submissive than a sheep. They passed me, and went into the cottage together, and I followed them. Mr. Allardyce sat down in the chair he had vacated a minute before, and Blowhard stood wheezing in the middle of the room, with his head bent forward, and his eyes roving from one to another of us. Two or three curious folks had already gathered about the door, and at my father's command I shut them out of sight and hearing.

'Now,' said Mr. Allardyce, addressing the unwilling guest, 'I want you to understand at once that it is in our power to send you and your fellow criminals to prison. I have consulted a friend of mine, who is eminent as a jurist, and he tells me that you are all liable to a sentence of anything from three to fourteen years.'

Blowhard's legs began to shake beneath him, and his knotted hands came together. As to what it was to be eminent as a jurist, I had no remotest beginning of a notion; but the words struck a kind of awe and admiration into me, and I can guess what they did with the culprit. I had never known a man of reading who could use a simpler Saxon than Mr. Allardyce, when he had a mind that way; but I suppose he meant to shake Old Blowhard's soul, and I am sure he did it.

'I never did you harm,' he went on. 'My friend Salter never

did you harm. You and your wicked companions set upon two defenceless men, whose only fault is that they were trying to do you good. Your only reason for your crime was that you could earn a miserable handful of shillings by it. You have earned the devil's money, and you have spent it in the devil's way. Are you any the better for it? You know you live your life in fear. You know you have not had a quiet hour since you took your blood-money in your guilty hand. You know that I could send you to gaol this minute. Now, what have you to say? '

A more cunning criminal than the wretched Blowhard might have seen a way to say something. He might have worn an air of astounded innocence. He might have blustered, or he might have whined. He might have suspected that the accuser was playing a game of bluff, and have bluffed back again. But Blowhard's knees were loosened and shaken, and his inwards were as water. He passed his hand across his wet forehead, and left three of four smeary lines in the dirt there, and he looked from one to the other of us, and wheezed heavily; but he had no answer, and, apparently, tried to find none.

' If you had killed us,' said Mr. Allardyce, ' and you went very near it, do you know what would have been done to you? '

Old Blowhard took the loose collar of his dirty shirt, and tugged at it as if it choked him. It was plain to see that he knew, and equally plain to see that the knowledge was unpleasant.

' Just so,' said Mr. Allardyce, interpreting the gesture. ' You have been within an inch of being hanged for murder.' He made a pause there, just to allow that idea to penetrate Old Blowhard's mind. ' And now,' he added, ' let me tell you something which you have not been able to know, or to find out for yourself. If this had happened in a great town, you and your fellow criminals, Tunley, Rusker, Ault, and Hotchkiss, would all have been in gaol long ago.'

He dropped the names slowly, one by one, and as each name fell on his ear, Blowhard's eyes widened and his jaw drooped, until the man looked all gaping mouth and gaping eyes. I never saw anything like him. He shook like a bush in the wind, and his face was as wet as if he had newly dipped it in water.

' But,' said Mr. Allardyce, ' Major Torvell, of Castle Barfield, is a personal friend of mine. It has cost me a great deal of trouble to keep him from arresting you five on suspicion. If he had done so, I should have been compelled by law to appear against you.'

Major Torvell's name, as old Barfield folk will still remember, was one to conjure with in those days. The Major—an old soldier of fortune, who had fought with mercenary Irish valour the wide world over, under half a score of flags—was dreaded ever since he had quelled the mining riots, and the Irish row in Union Alley; and any man who could boast his personal friendship was to be feared by any criminal within twenty miles, though a dozen big or biggish towns lay within that radius. If anything could have added to Blowhard's terror the mention of that magic name would have done it.

'You are all married men,' said Mr. Allardyce; 'you all have children. I shall be glad to spare you if I can. Meet me here to-morrow with Ault and Tunley and Hotchkiss and Rusker, and I shall see if you are fit to be forgiven. Come at twelve o'clock. Now you may go.'

He went blindly, like a drunken man, smearing his sweating hand across his wet forehead.

'Well,' said father, with a long breath, 'I'd rather spend my life in gaol than ha' that to go through with.'

Mr. Allardyce nodded by way of answer. He was very weak and tired, and now that the excitement was over for the time, he was white to the lips. He got back into his hired carriage with difficulty, and was driven away.

CHAPTER IX

WHAT means Old Blowhard took to bring his men together I never knew, but on the following day he turned up at noon, still looking horribly scared, and with him came the man with the cleft palate, who answered to the name of Rusker. When Mr. Allardyce came, punctual to the hour, only those two were present, but in a little while the others slouched in, amidst the wondering looks of the neighbours, who knew as well as we did that these men were suspected.

Mr. Allardyce made us all kneel down. He prayed for those blackguards with a tender and holy zeal; he besought God to touch their cruel and hardened hearts, and to bring them to contrition. How they felt I can only guess, but they gave no sign of ruth. They merely looked awkward and very ill at ease, and I fancy the idea uppermost in such poor minds as they had was, that they were being let off at an unexpectedly cheap rate. Such emotion as there was of the sort Mr. Allardyce wished to awaken, was all on the side of the injured, I am sure, and if my judgement should for the moment seem uncharitable, you may mark how the sequel justified it.

We had nothing to lock up in our poor house, and so our door had neither bolt nor bar to it; and we had scarce risen from our knees, when without warning in broke upon us Mr. Joseph Brambler followed by Mr. Jeremiah in a tall hat of antique fashion and a pair of false collars, the loose strings of which meandered down his back.

'Hillo!' said Mr. Brambler, looking round in amazement. What's this? Is it a love-feast, or what is it?'

Mr. Allardyce, who knew Mr. Brambler well, shook hands with

him, and, taking him aside, spoke to him in a low tone for half a minute.

Mr. Brambler's face was turned towards mine, and I could read on it an expression of complete amazement at the first. This gave way to a look of wrath, and by-and-by he drove one clenched hand into the palm of the other, and said 'No!' like the snap of a pistol shot.

'But, my dear friend——' said Mr. Allardyce.

'Niver! niver! niver!' cried Mr. Brambler; and struggling from the clergyman, who strove to keep him in the corner to which he had led him, he faced my father, his visage red with anger, and his white hair and whiskers seeming to bristle. 'Jack Salter,' he began, in such wrath that he could hardly speak, 'do you mean to tell me—do *you* mean to tell *me*——' He was in such a rage that he boggled and stammered at almost every word. 'What! You'm i' the same tale wi' the parson? You! as I've helped and nourished, an'—an'—an' nutrified. D'ye mean to tell *me* that?'

He stared about him in an exasperation which was at least half made up of bewilderment.

'I'm leavin' the matter in Mr. Allardyce's hands, sir,' said father.

'You've *got* these damn rascals here,' cried Mr. Brambler, 'with not a man among 'em with the cheek to deny his guilt, an' you're agoin' to let 'em off?'

'It's Mr. Allardyce's wish,' said father.

'Look here, gaffer!' cried Mr. Brambler, turning on the curate, 'do you mean to tell me as this is Christian doctrine? A parcel o' murderous vagabonds like that!'

'We pray,' said Mr. Allardyce, 'that our trespasses may be forgiven, even as we forgive those who trespass against us.'

'Oh!' said Mr. Brambler, clutching at his hair; 'I'm mad!'

The gesture knocked his hat off, and it fell to the floor. I picked it up and held it out to him, but he took no notice of it or me, but stood as if rooted to the floor, with both hands tugging at his respectable, close-cropped white hair.

'Our Jerry!' he said, appealing to his brother, who stood there with his fatuous under lip drooping and his gooseberry eyes wide open. 'I'm mad! That's what's the matter wi' me.'

The five detected criminals who had come here to be pardoned and sent about their business were all huddled together in one corner of the room, and looked on with blank faces. Here was an opposition upon which they had not counted.

'My dear friend——' Mr. Allardyce began again; but Mr. Brambler cut him short once more.

'Call yourself a Christian?' he cried. 'Call yourself a parson? Let a crowd o' villians like that loose o' the world. Why, it's a crime. It's enough to bring a judgement on the 'ouse!'

At this extreme statement of the case my father laughed, and Mr. Brambler turned on him as if stricken with amazement.

'Our Jerry!' he said, once more appealing to his brother. 'This is the cove I've fed and cockered up ever since he got mauled at the hands of these fellers. D'ye hear him now?'

Mr. Jeremiah, who was wholly in the dark, stared vacantly and said nothing.

'Look here,' said Mr. Joseph Brambler, standing with his feet wide apart and both hands outspread—'look here, Jack Salter: what was it d'ye think, as made me so fond o' *you* all on a sudden? D'ye think I've got nothin' else to do wi' my money than spend it on a chap as'll turn round the very fust chance he gets, an' flouts me to my face?'

'I don't understand, Mr. Brambler,' said father, with a puzzled look.

'Don't understand?' retorted Mr. Brambler. 'No, nor me naything, nor nobody else.'

All this time I had been holding out his hat towards him. He saw it suddenly, pounced upon it, and set to work to dust it so savagely, that he made a great dent in the crown. Then he slammed it on his head and sat down, a very picture of exasperation.

I think we were all as much astonished at him as he appeared to be at us, for none of us could guess why Mr. Allardyce's plan of pardon affected him at all.

It was Mr. Jeremiah who enlightened us.

'Gentlemen,' said Mr. Jeremiah, 'I niver *was* a Don at understandin' things, but what's this all about?'

'About?' ejaculated his brother, and repeated the word with an accent which seemed to imply that it conveyed some new affront to him. 'About? Why, here's Parson Allardyce a-tellin' me as these chaps here had as good as confessed as it was them as set about him and this here Jack Salter. And now he's for lettin' them off with a prayer and a sermon. 'I'll sermon 'em!'

'Mr. Brambler,' said Mr. Allardyce, in his most persuasive manner, 'you have behaved with so much kindness in this matter already—you have shown such a spirit of Christian benevolence——'

'Christian benevolence be blowed!' said Mr. Brambler fiercely. 'There's no Christian benevolence about me. No, thank you. I niver was one o' that sort, the Lord be praised!'

'Ye see,' said Mr. Jeremiah, addressing himself to the bewildered clergyman, 'there's somebody behind these chaps. They fired the bullet to be sure, but who loaded the gun? If you let 'em off, how are you goin' to get at him? That's what Mr. Joseph wants to know.'

'Yes,' said Mr. Joseph, rising and slapping his hat soundingly with his open palm; 'that's what Mr. Joseph wants to know. A low-bred blaggard as has done more to bring the trade into bad repute than any ten men in the countryside. A feller as has had the cheek to talk to me on 'Change at Birmingham, cuss him! You know who I mean!' he cried, advancing with a threatening hand on the huddled five. 'Who paid the dirty money for the dirty work?'

It was a curious thing to see that murderous gang which had been so bold in the dark two months ago all striving to hide one behind the other before this truculent little gray old man.

But, then, Mr. Joseph Brambler was the biggest man in the local trade, and these poor wretches were like ants before him.

'I know him!' cried Mr. Brambler, shaking his hand in Blowhard's face. 'Ay! I know him as well as you do. It matters naught to me whether you rot in gaol or out of it, but if you are to be let off, goo an' tell the man I know him. Look here, you cowardly rats, five pound and a free pardon to any man of you as'll tell the truth —five pound, money down!'

He thrust one hand into his trouser pocket and brought it out full of gold and silver. Two or three coins fell from the little brimming heap, but he took no notice of them in his excitement.

'That!' he cried, 'for any man as'll speak the truth and swear to it in a court afore a judge.'

They all looked at him, and they all looked greedy-eyed at the money; and they all looked at one another.

That mutual glance daunted them all, and not one made a move. If the offer had been made to any one of them alone it would of course been instantly accepted. But Mr .Brambler's zeal and passion defeated themselves, as zeal and passion very often do.

He stood with the money in his hand for a full minute, looking from face to face, but they all avoided his eye after the first glance, and he thrust the bribe back again into his pocket with a curse which even the clergyman's presence could not repress.

I had gone on hands and knees to hunt the fallen coins, and having by this time gathered them, I stood up to hand them to him.

In his petulance he struck my arm so sharply as to send the money tinkling and rolling about the room again.

'Mr. Allardyce,' he said, restraining himself after this outburst, and trying to speak calmly, 'I want to know if you think you'm acting like a man in this affair. You've suffered by this piece o' divilry yourself, an' I should ha' thought even a parson ud ha' had more sperit. I've known that man—the man as set these chaps to work on you and this Jack Salter here—I've known that man for 'ears an' 'ears. He's a grinder o' the faces o' the poor. He's a bitter enemy to many, an' a friend to none. He's set himself agen me these 'ears past. He's had the face to cheek me in the presence of a hunderd, tho' I've showed him I despised him, an' wouldn't ha' soiled my feet by wiping 'em on his coat with him inside it.'

'"Vengeance is mine,"' quoted Mr. Allardyce, '"I will repay saith the Lord."'

'Oh,' said Mr. Joseph Brambler, 'keep that for the pulpit. That's all right in its proper place, no doubt.'

'We will talk at another place and another time, Mr. Brambler,' said the clergyman. 'But the law of God is not made for the pulpit and for Sundays only; it is meant to rule every action and every moment of our lives. You will hardly deny that Salter and myself were the sufferers in this matter, and if we feel it our duty as Christian men to forgive——'

'Oh, Rubbidge!' cried Mr. Brambler. 'It's a wicked crime, and that's all theer is to be said about it. Look at 'em! D'ye think you'll iver make saints an' angels o' that lot?'

'They are men like ourselves,' Mr. Allardyce responded. 'They are our unhappy brothers.'

'Here, our Jerry,' said Mr. Joseph, redder in the face than ever, 'come along out o' this afore I lose my temper.'

He made for the door, but paused and turned with his hand on the catch.

'You stick to this newly-fangled nonsense, Jack Salter?'

'I'm with Mr. Allardyce, sir,' said father. 'I must follow where he leads.'

'Very well,' retorted Mr. Joseph bitterly. 'I've been the best friend you iver had, but I dessay you can get along without me now.'

'You've done me great kindness, sir,' said father, 'more than anybody iver did in all my life. I can niver forget it, niver; but I'm bound to follow Mr. Allardyce.'

'All right,' cried Mr. Brambler, 'theer's a pair on ye! Good-bye to both, for a pair o' snivellin' nincompoops.'

With that he banged the door open, and calling anew on 'our Jerry,' he walked into the road, mounted the dog-cart in which he had arrived, and drove away with his brother.

'Mr. Allardyce,' said mother, 'do you see what you've done? You've drove away my man's best friend.'

'Well, well, my wench,' said father gently, 'we must try to mek the best on it. As for these chaps, Mr. Allardyce, I'm none eager for my part to tek revenge upon 'em. What I've done since I had the means by your good help to do it, sir, has been to spend myself heart and soul for their welfare. They know that, sir, as well as you an' me know it. They're a poor ignorant lot, and a drop o' beer is worth a fellow creetur's life to 'em. As you said yourself, just now, sir, they've all got wives an' children to the parish. I niver set up to be much of a Christian, and I'll mek no pretences. Since you say let 'em go, I say let 'em go. I shouldn't ha' done it if I'd been alone, but they handled you bad, as they did me, an' it was just your bein' with me at the minute as let you in for it at all. It was for you to speak, sir, an' you've said the word, and I say ditto to it.'

'Go home, men,' said Mr. Allardyce. 'I shall pray that your hearts may be softened, and that you may become better men for this forgiveness.'

He had, on Mr. Brambler's departure, closed the door to shut out the curious neighbours who were still congregated outside, and now he reopened it, and stood on one side to let them file out.

'Is theer a man among ye?' my mother demanded. 'Is theer one as'll say so much as "Thank you"?'

They looked shiftily about at this appeal, but none of them spoke and after hanging undeterminately for a minute or two, they slouched away hangdog and downcast, each man pulling his frowsy cap on to his frowsy head with both hands as he went out, as if the act were laborious and weighty, and demanded the exercise of great strength.

I stood on tiptoe to look after them through the window, and saw them wander slowly through the little crowd, speaking to nobody and looking at nobody, but all staring gloomily at the roadway, and looking very much more like men who had been sentenced to a term of penal servitude than like men who had just had a merciful and unlooked-for escape.

When they had all gone, my mother sat down suddenly on the side of the bed and threw her coarse apron over her face, and began to rock to and fro.

'It's nothin', sir,' said father. 'She's a bit upset, but that'll pass. I shall be about again, as well and strong as iver, in a day or two. When I can get as far, I'll mek it my business to pay my duty to you, Mr. Allardyce.'

'You have shown mercy, Salter,' said Mr. Allardyce, grasping him by the hand. 'Perhaps in that supreme hour when all men have most need of mercy, you may think of this day with comfort.'

With that he went away. As he mounted into the open fly, in which he had come to us, he shuddered and gave a sick sort of gasp. The brick-kilns were burning opposite, and their filthy smell was heavier on the air than common, so that even I felt some repulsion at it, though I had been born in that abominable atmosphere. He smiled a second later, as much as to say that it was over; but, watch ing him from the doorway, I saw that he was fain to draw out his handkerchief and hide his mouth and nostrils in it.

Young as I was, I remember, in a dim way, wondering that a gentleman who could afford to live where and how he would (for how in those ignorant childish days, should I associate poverty with a clergyman?) should care to come to such a place as this at all.

I was not, so far as I know, touched by any sense of magnanimity in that morning's conduct. I had wondered, and had been interested and now that I have been recalling the scene so closely in my own mind I seem to have had a curious understanding of the widely varying frames of mind of the people who had taken part in it, but very few things in the conduct of their elders are surprising to children. It looked natural, simply and purely because it had all happened, and since father said it was right, it was right as a matter of course and there was an end to it.

Our neighbours, who were not very much moved by respect for anybody's privacy, got into our doorway, and stared over one another's shoulders into the room.

Father quietly, and without a word, closed the door upon them and they yielded to the gentle pressure he used; but some of them went to the window and flattened their noses against it, in their desire to see what was going on. Father went out and dispersed them in a way which for him was rather pettish. Then he came back again, and sat down with a wistful look at mother, who was still rocking to and fro.

'Thou'rt not vexed wi' me, lass? ' he asked at length, rising and laying a hand upon her shoulder.

'Vexed wi' thee, lad? ' she answered, without uncovering her face. 'Nay, I'm none vexed with thee.'

'It's a thing to be thought on,' said my father, after a long pause, but it seems to me as Mr. Allardyce's doctrine's a deal too soft for this world. Theer's no manner of a doubt as he's got the Scripters for it, howiver, an' it's true enough that if everybody was like him, the world 'ud be mended clean out o' knowledge.'

'Oh, Jack! Jack! ' cried my mother, rising suddenly, and throwing both arms about his neck. 'Thou'rt the best man i' the world.'

'Not I, lass,' he answered, laughing, 'but if it does thee good to think, think it. I've done no more than the parson, and without him, I should niver so much as thought on it.'

'The parson! ' cried mother. 'It's his business; but theer's no other man than thee, Jack, as iver I've set eyes on as'd ha' listened to him. He's right, Jack—he's right. When thy time comes, thou'lt die easier for this day's work. But, oh, lad! it cut me cruel hard first. To think what thou wast like when they carried thee in here, wi' thy poor face all boltered wi' blood an' mire, and to think as them villins was the ones as did it. I could ha' took the life of every one on 'em wi' my own hand. I felt like it. It's agen thee grain to let 'em off, but you'm right, Jack, an' I'll love thee for it, an' respect thee for it, to my dyin' day. An' if I'm iver crank again, or out o' temper, I'll think o' thee this day.'

'Eh, my pretty wench,' he answered, kissing her, 'I'm glad thou'rt o' the same mind, for I'm not altogether that sure an' certain o' the rights on it as I should like to be. Mercy's a fine thing, but theer's summat in a man's heart as calls out for justice too. I've no such hope as Mr. Allardyce seems to find in his own mind—no such hope at all. Theer's no more gratefulness or thankfulness in the hearts o' them chaps than there is in that ode kettle.'

'I'm none so sure o' that,' said mother.

'Ay, ay,' said father; 'but I bin. Why, my wench, I feel it here as if it was spoke out of Holy Writ. If I'd done a thing such as was done to me, an' been insulted by a pardon for it, I should be ripe for murder. I should ha' called for justice as my rights. "Yis," I'd ha' said, "I done it. You've fun me out, an' I'm here to tek the consequences!" But to sneak on two men in the dark, more than two to one, to batter 'em to a jelly under the shelter o' the night, and then to stand up an' tek pardon for it, an' to be dismissed as if they wasn't worth our punishin'—why, my dear gell, a man as is made i' that way's no man at all. They'll nurse a bitter spite agen Mr. Allardyce an' me as long as theer's a breath left in their miserable bodies.'

'You didn't think i' that way when you let 'em off?' cried mother in dismay.

'Ay, but I did, my wench,' he answered. 'They'd no feelin' agen me at the beginnin', nor agen the parson neither. They was bribed to do it. What's a man's life agen a bellyfull o' beer for such cattle as that? But now they'll hate us both, for we've made 'em despisable to their own hearts.'

'I hope they're none so wicked,' mother said, with all her enthusiasm sadly dashed.

‘I’d like to hope that too, my lass,’ father answered.

The argument ended there. Mother went quietly about her household duties, and father took a book from the one little shelf which held his literary treasures. They were mostly, if not all, gifts from Mr. Allardyce, and were not frivolous things, such as a woman or a child would care to look at, but good, hard, headachy literature of the politico-economic sort. Amongst the rest I remember a copy of the Truck Act, and a big Parliamentary Blue Book, which contained the evidence given before a Commission by people interested in the coal and iron trade, and the Commission’s report upon the evidence. I myself sometimes burrowed in these, and got an occasional ray of partial understanding of their meaning; but nobody can fancy what I thought of my father’s power and erudition.

The household had been all quiet for half an hour, and I was busy with slate and pencil, when my mother suddenly made an exclamation, and stooping to the floor, picked up a half-crown.

When Mr. Joseph Brambler had sent his own money flying out of my hand it had been in my mind to pick it up again, and set it on the table for him; but I had grown so intensely interested in what was going on that I had forgotten all about it, and there the money still lay on the floor, most of it hidden under the bed. I crawled about on hands and knees until I was satisfied that I had found it all. There was seven and sixpence in silver, and there was one golden sovereign, quite a mine of wealth to my mind.

‘That must go to Mr. Brambler,’ said my father, when he had counted it over. ‘I doubt if I’ve the strength to walk as far. I darn’t try it. Jack, see if thou hast a pocket without a hole in it.’

‘He’ll find no pocket *with* a hole in it, I’ll go bail,’ said mother, with one of her occasional touches of tartness.

‘That’s well,’ said father, in his placid way. ‘If theer’s such a thing as a bit o’ clean rag to wrap it up in, he’d carry it safer.’

My mother found the bit of clean rag and sewed the money in it, and with her own hand pushed it deep into my pocket, the bottom of which she explored carefully to see if her boast were good.

‘Now put your hand on that,’ she said, ‘an’ keep it theer, an’ niver loose that money till you hand it to Mr. Brambler. An’ don’t you stop to play wi’ nobody, an’ don’t change a word wi’ nobody, unless it's to say "Good-day." And now be off, an' come straight back again.'

Thus charged, I set out mightily inflated with the sense of my own importance in being trusted with such a prodigious sum of money. I clutched the treasure until it was moist and hot in my hand, and I ran until I was fairly winded, so that when I arrived at Mr. Brambler's gate I had to hold on to it for a while to recover breath.

Whilst I was panting there, Mr. Brambler came round the corner of the house in a linen jacket and a straw hat, and carrying a rake over one shoulder and a hoe across the other.

'Well,' he said, deliberately disburdening himself of his gardening tools and propping them against the wall, 'what's your business?'

He was no longer the friendly personage he had been, but looked at me with a sour and disconcerting visage.

'If you please, sir,' I said holding out the little parcel, 'this is the money you dropped in our kitchen.'

'Oh!' said Mr. Brambler, and looked at me as sternly as before.

He took out a penknife and cut the few cotton threads by which my mother had secured the packet, and as he did so, I had a glimpse of Jane in her spotless print dress and her white cap, and I thought of the times I had had under that rosy damsel's protection, and it was borne in upon me that those times were over, and the policy of forgiving Old Blowhard and his gang, and estranging Mr. Joseph Brambler looked poor and thin indeed.

'I dropped that, did I?' said Mr. Brambler, when he had counted the money. 'Who sent it, do you say?'

'Father and mother, if you please, sir.'

'Well,' said he, 'they're honest people, an' that's something to say for 'em. Hungry, eh?'

'Not very, please, sir.'

'Oh, not very! Not so hungry as you was when you come here first, eh?'

'Oh no, sir.'

'Well, can you heat a meal?' he asked.

I thought I could.

‘ Then come in, an’ shut the gate behind you. Jane, find a mouthful for this here young Salter.’

Jane had always shown a positive pleasure in ministering to my wants, and she set about her task as willingly as ever. But first I was sent to the kitchen sink to wash my hands and face, which were grimy with dust and perspiration, and whilst I was engaged I seemed to know that Mr. Brambler was staring very hard at me from behind. The instinct was true enough, for whenever I took a glance at him, I caught his eye.

When Jane had set out the clean white napkin on the clean scoured table, and had put out a plate, and a knife and fork, and a salt-cellar, and a knobbly loaf, and then one of those big meat-pies which seemed to be a staple dish in Mr. Brambler's household, he was still looking at me as hard as ever.

‘ It's no fault o’ yourn, I reckon,’ he said at last, ‘ but you've got a fool for a father.’

What prompted me to that awful deed of courage I cannot tell, but I stood bolt upright, and said:

‘ No, I haven't.’

‘ You haven't, haven't you? ’ said Mr. Brambler.

‘ My father's a wise man,’ I answered hotly, ‘ an’ he's the best man in the world.’

‘ Who says so? ’ he asked.

‘ Mother does,’ I retorted.

‘ Well,’ said Mr. Brambler, with a return of his old good-humour, ‘ that settles it. Now pitch into your dinner.’

I pitched into my dinner rather feebly, for I felt hurt and offended, and not even meat-pie could soothe me.

When at last a lump of pie encountered somehow with a lump of injured sentiment in my throat, I began to cry, and Mr. Brambler took to patting me on the back.

‘ Theer, theer,’ he said kindly, ‘ say no more about it. Here's a shillin’ for thee.’

I was soon pacified, for want and hunger will make even a child mercenary, and in those days I thought nothing so valuable as money, though I have changed my mind since then. I ate as much as I wanted, and my host stood and watched me all the while.

When at last I pushed my plate away, and got down from my chair, Mr. Brambler asked me, with great solemnity, if I could take a message.

I said that I thought I could.

'Very well, then,' he said, 'tell your father as him an' me is just as good friends as ever. Tell him as him an' Parson Allardyce is the biggest brace o' fools I ever heerd tell on, an' tell him I wish theer was more like 'em. Now, just say that over.'

No. I wouldn't say it over; I couldn't say it over, and since to owe allegiance and not to give it, and to keep the shilling at the same time, seemed impossible, I put the shining coin upon the table, though it brought tears to my cheek to do it.

'Well,' said Mr. Brambler, 'you'm a queer lot, to be sure. Here! I'll write a bit of a note for you. Put that shillin' in your pocket.'

I was glad enough to obey him, and he went away for a few minutes. When he came back he put an envelope into my jacket-pocket, and patted me on the back. When I got home I gave my father the letter, and he read it aloud:

'JOHN SALTER,

'You and me are as good friends as ever. You and Parson Allardyce are the biggest brace of fools I ever met, and I wish there was more like you.

JOSEPH BRAMBLER.'

'Now,' said father, slapping the open letter as it lay on the table before him, 'theer, just for once in a way, is a man.'

CHAPTER X

THE episode just narrated brought about one result which, when one comes to look at it, was natural enough. Long after his association with Mr. Allardyce, my father had never been what one would call a religious man; but this business set him thinking about the ethics of Christianity, and in a month or two he joined a body known as the Primitive Christians, and became a preacher among them. They believed, so far as I remember, in a community of goods amongst themselves, though I never heard that they made any greater parade in the way of practice than other sections of the Christian Church. They were pledged to peace in all ways, and looked on armies and navies, even for purposes of defence, as forbidden and unlawful. In short, they put plain meaning to plain words, and they were, so far as I knew them, a respectable and even admirable body of cranks and enthusiasts.

It was through his association with this little congregation of men and women that the great libel case came off. At the meetings of the Primitive Christians discussions were held with 'the Gentiles,' and these were sometimes managed in a fashion which would at that time of day have deserved to be called unparliamentary. For the fighting instinct is not wholly to be destroyed in a man, even when he turns Christian, and makes himself as primitive as he can, and the outsiders were certainly sometimes provocative of wrath.

We used to meet in a little chapel in a lane just off the highroad, about half way between our cottage and Barfield High Street. A filthy open gutter ran on either side the lane, and at the end of it a chemical factory sent out loathsome odours. The water in the kennels was so foul that it never froze even in the hardest weather, and in the summer time it was a wonder that it did not breed a pestilence. The wretched lane looked as if it had never once been swept and garnished since first the land which made it had been fenced in with houses. It was strewn everywhere with nameless rubbish, and since it was too narrow for side-paths, the approaches to the few houses in it, and to our chapel, bridged the gutters with small arches of brick.

We were too poor to pay a salaried minister, and I am not quite sure that such an employment would not have been contrary to our tenets. I doubt very much if a benefice of any sort would have been looked upon as primitive. I know it was not reckoned primitive to have a pulpit, and that the amateur orators, and the disputants, harangued us from the floor.

There was a public-house immediately behind, which held a licence to brew upon the premises, and the odour of the brewing will at any moment bring the shabby familiar little old place before me as if I saw it once again with bodily eyes, as I never shall. It is down, long ago, and the very lane it stood in has almost perished out of memory.

I think that but for the half hour devoted to discussion after evening service on Sundays we should never have made but a small gathering, but this enjoyed a certain amount of popularity. The unfriendly disputants generally came from a distance—some from Birmingham, some from Wolverhampton. The smaller towns do not breed that kind of man. A good many of them were very young, and none of them, I suspect, was over the rank of shopman or shopboy; but they looked distinguished among our poorer crowd, and were loud in neckties and sham jewellery, and brilliant with hair-oil. It comes easy to believe now that they were an ignorant lot, but they made a great show of learning, and one young man used to talk about the original Greek and Hebrew in a way which fairly frightened me. I dare say that if anybody had been competent to question him, he would have turned out to know as much about the original Greek and Hebrew as I did; but he was very confident and fluent, and often seemed to bear down opposition, and to leave simple souls perplexed.

I remember that on one occasion a doddering old man was proclaiming very clumsily his belief that so long as a man was sincere the form of his belief mattered nothing. The young gentleman I have in my mind knocked him into a cocked hat, by declaring that the word 'sincere' was derived from *sin,* without, and *ciro,* wax, and that if he did not change his faith pretty smartly, he would not be long without wax, for his immortal fate would be 'ermetically sealed. This combination of learning and lively badinage set the young man on a pedestal among his compeers.

My father could never be persuaded to enter into these wrangles, though he spoke often on the plain duties of life, and, most of all, the common duties of mutual help and patience. He was talking thus one bitter cold night, when the stone floor of the little chapel was like ice, and I was cramped up, a mere bundle of shivers, with pins and needles in my feet and legs, and trying to imagine that their discomfort made me warmer, when the door opened with a bitter gust of wind, a clumsy step sounded heavy on the floor, and my father paused suddenly in the very middle of a word, and stared before him with a questioning, short-sighted look, which sent every glance in the room on a search in the direction of his own.

The place was feebly illuminated by two small gas-jets, which gave barely as much light as a couple of rushlights would have afforded, and these being behind the newcomer, threw his face and figure into shadow, or, to speak more exactly, left them mingled with the common shadows of the room. My young eyes, however, had little difficulty in identifying the intruder as Mr. Sim, who had deposited his burly figure on a form at the back of the chapel, and sat there balancing a silk hat between both hands, and waving his head in a circular fashion, whilst he looked straight in front of him, as if he had been in a kind of dreamy trance.

I was not long in deciding that Mr. Sim was drunk, for, unhappily, drunken men were common in my experience, and I knew the signs already.

Mr. Sim, having been well stared at by the whole congregation, sat there waving and looking vacantly in front of him, without seeming to see anything, and my father pulled himself together, and pursued his discourse.

I had been so occupied in thinking how cold I was, and how the pins and needles would sting when I had to stand up at the singing of the hymn, that I knew little of the subject matter of his discourse, but I had a vague idea that he had fallen upon a favourite topic of his, and was lamenting the cruelty of oppressions in general, and the oppression of his own class in particular; but from the moment when Mr. Sim entered, I heard every word. There were men, he went on to say, who made a trade of oppression, and who grew fat and throve on it.

I screwed round in my corner, and watched Mr. Sim like one fascinated, and I saw him rise unsteadily, and bat his eyes as if he were trying to clear his obfuscated sight.

'That thee, Jack Salter? ' he asked, with a hiccup.

And the small congregation turned, indignant and amazed at the interruption.

'Silence in the Lord's house! ' said one of the Primitives, but Mr. Sim did not appear to have heard him.

'They tode me as I should find thee here,' he said, and sat down with such suddeness that he was only saved from falling by a clutch on either side.

'I'm to be found at most times pretty easy,' said father; 'but we can have no disturbance here.'

An indignant murmur from the congregation confirmed this, and Mr. Sim sat quiet for a minute or two.

'Now, in illustration of what I've been a-sayin',' my father went on, 'tek the case o' the Black Country nailer. Theer's not a soul i' this congregation as doesn't know the iniquities they suffer under. Theer are them amongst the foggers as keep three sets of weights—one to buy with from the wretched nailer, one to sell with to the wretched nailer, and one to show the inspector when he comes his rounds. One of these sets is heavy, an' the other's light, an' th' only just weights i' the place are them as are never used. Now, my brethren, it is written in that Book which we have chose to live and die by that a fause weight is an abomination to the Lord. But here, in the case I speak of, is not a single lie an' a single crime, but a tribble lie an' a tribble crime. In the day when Heaven measures out its justice to sinful man, how shall he stand who all the days of his man'ood has lived that tribble lie and flourished on that tribble crime? '

Mr. Sim at this stood bolt upright, for the moment half sobered.

'Bist talkin' at me, Jack Salter? ' he demanded.

'At thee,' my father retorted fiercely, 'an' ten out of ivery score of all thy wicked tribe.'

'I'll mak thee prove thy words! ' cried Sim. 'As sure as theer's law in the land, I'll mak thee prove thy words! '

'Theer are them,' said my father, in that deep-mouthed ringing voice which, more than anything else, made him a power as an orator before the mob—'theer are them who, bein' denounced for their extortions, an' findin' no place to hide from public shame, have paid blood-money—have bought at the hands of hired villains the life of a man vowed to God's service, an' the life of a commoner, poorer man as strove to free his fellow-men from the slavery they was born an' bred in, to take the bitter cup o' misery from their lips an' the bitter bread o' slavery from their hands, to offer 'em the meat of independence an' the wine o' freedom. And in the house o' God Himself one such sinner shall hear the word o' truth, an' the fear o' the God he has offended an' the law he has defied shall thunder in his soul. Think ye God is hoodwinked? Think ye the heavens are blind? No, I tell ye. Go to your bed, and let that truth rankle in your heart till terror breeds repentance, an' repentance brings forgiveness.'

I have written the words as nearly as I can recall them, but I cannot set the voice on paper, pealing deep and stern, and unmarred for any ear that heard it by the broad mid-England dialect it uttered, nor can I write the flashing eye, and the white, exalted face, and the terrible gesture of the denouncing hand. Nor was the great voice stern all through, for it melted into pity when he spoke of the sufferings he knew so well and had endured so long.

Sim stood under it impotent to arrest the torrent, but swept along by it, and, as it were, half-drowned in it.

'Is that for me, too, Jack Salter? ' he asked at length.

'Ay, lad,' said my father, 'an', wisely taken, it's the kindest word thou hast listened to sence thy poor mother died.'

'Good! ' said Mr. Sim, without a sign of drink upon him. 'I know a goodish many o' the people here. I know thee, 'Saiah Winter, and thee, Bill Guest, an' thee, Bob Truman.'

He named perhaps a dozen, peering here and there in the dim light in his heavy, over-fed way.

'You'll hear o' this again, Salter,' he continued. 'You've put your neck i' the noose this time, my lad.'

He went out in a much steadier fashion than he had entered, and my father brought his address to an abrupt conclusion. One very ancient Primitive—the father of the flock, I think he was—gave out the Doxology, two lines at a time, and then somebody pronounced a long benediction; but nobody's heart was in the business any further, and all were eager to discuss the strange event of the evening.

Father stayed for a little while only, and then led me home, but I learned enough to know that he was considered to have done a very dangerous thing.

He talked to me as we went home about it.

'I spoke not a word but the truth, Jack,' said he. 'Don't say a word to frighten mother. Her's got enough to bear a'ready, poor thing!'

There was little need for either of us to tell her, for the next day the whole district seemed to be on fire with the news. Jack Salter, the Preaching Nailer, as they called him, had publicly charged Mr. Sim with subornation of murder, and Mr. Sim was going to have the law on him. This charivari filled me with a dreadful fear, but I felt it exalting too, and rejoiced in the added importance it gave me.

Very early in the morning my father went out to see Mr. Allardyce, and, as I learned afterwards, to consult him on the matter, and in the afternoon, Mr. Joseph Brambler drove down in a state of high excitement. My father was barely home again when Mr. Brambler arrived, and all the inhabitants of our row, to the very babies, turned out to look at him and his dogcart, and to speculate on the events which were taking place inside our house.

'I've heard all about it, Salter,' cried Mr. Brambler, 'and if the tale as I'm told it should turn out to be true, you've played the man, an' I'll stick by you—ay, I will, lad, if it costs me a hundred pound—or two, for that matter!'

'I've seen Mr. Allardyce, sir,' said father, 'an' he's promised all he can do if Mr. Sim carries his threat out. But he thinks that seems an onlikely sort o' thing to happen. I'm as ignorant o' the law as a man can easy be, but, as I learn from Mr. Allardyce, theer's two ways as Sim can go in. He could go agen me for damages, but then theer's little use in that in the case of a man as poor as I be. Then he can mak' it a charge o' what Mr. Allardyce says is called criminal, and if I was fun' guilty that'd mean imprisonment.'

'Well, Salter,' said the great man, 'you shan't want for lawyer's help an' that you can mak' up your mind to. I'll find that for you if it should be needed. But I should count that Sim's too poor sperited to dare to carry the story into court, and beyond that Salter, he's too near the fire not to be a little bit afeard o' bein' singed. You spoke up about the weights, I'm told.'

'Yes, sir,' said father, 'I had a word to say about it.'

'I'll nail him theer,' declared Mr. Brambler. 'I'll set th' inspector on to him this instant minute.'

He was so fired with his idea that he was out of the house like a rocket, and, jumping like a young man into his dog-cart, he drove away at full speed, shouting out that he would be back as soon as he had 'set them wheels a-workin'.'

Mr. Brambler was so very big a man, indeed, amongst the nailers, that their ignorant minds could hardly conceive of anybody bigger. There were no local gentry, nor likely to be, within a mile or two of us, and so we had nobody to compare with him. He was far and away the most prosperous and the largest buyer of our products and his repeated presence under our roof gave me at least a sense of personal magnificence which hardly anything else in the world could then have conveyed to me.

He was away a couple of hours, and when he returned it was twilight; but father lit a candle to talk to him, and his eyes glittered and his face was rosy with triumph.

'Nothin' could ha' turned out better,' he declared. 'I lighted by chance at the Guest Arms, an' who should be there but th' inspector o' weights an' measures. We had a glass together, an' I put him up to the business.

'"Why, yes," he says, "it almost seems to be a custom o' the trade hereabouts," he says; "but they're hard to light on," he says.'

'"That," I says, "is because you work your rounds too regular. They send word to one another when you're on the move,"'

'"Well," he says, "it's a big district, an' if I didn't use some sort o' system with it, I should niver get through with the work," ' he says.

' " Well," says I, " just tak' a saunter across to old Sim's place right now," I says, " and see what you'll find theer." '

' So he walks acrost the road, and in a minute or two I follows him; an' theer he was i' Sim's ware'us, with Sim a-swearin' like a madman, threatenin' to have the law agen him, an' talkin' I don't know what sort o' foolishness. Th' inspector took it all pretty cool, as you may guess, an' theer, under the counter, we fun' all three sets o' weights. Th' inspector turned him out of his own ware'us an' locked the door, while he sent for a cart to carry 'em away.'

' " I dar' you to lay a hand upon my property," says Sim. " Them weights belongs to me." '

' " That's wheer it is," says the inspector. " That's what I'm impoundin' 'em for," ' he says.

' Oh, he's a rare chap for a ready tongue.

' " You owe that to Jack Salter," I says to Sim; and " Yes," says he, " I owe more than that to Jack Salter, an' I'll pay him yet." So I gi'en him a bit o' my mind, an', says I, " Bring your action," I says, " an' if money's wanted money's to be had. I'll back the man as showed you up," I says, " if it costs me five hundred pound." '

Father was not at all elated by this recital, and I think Mr. Brambler was a little disappointment in his quietude.

' I'm glad they've pounced on him at last,' he said. ' I bear no malice agen the man, Mr. Brambler, but he's been a public henemy these many 'ears, an' it's full time he l'arned his lesson.'

' He'll learn it! ' cried Mr. Brambler, an' I'll help him to learn it. Salter, I've had my knife in that chap this twenty year an' more. Mind ye, I'm Stafford, I am. Wheer I've got a likin' theer I stick to my friend; wheer I've got a mislikin' theer I stick to my henemy. Warm friend, warm henemy. That's my motto, Salter, an' depend on it, it's a good un.'

' It isn't Bible teachin', Mr. Brambler,' said father.

' Bible teachin'! ' cried the other. ' Oh, I forgot; theest been run away with by the parson. No, lad, niver mind Bible teachin'. A eye for a eye, an' tooth for a tooth's good enough Bible teachin' for me. Let a man carry his cup upright, an' refrain from damagin' his neighbour, an' he wants no Bible teachin'! '

‘I’m thinkin’,’ said father, ‘this is like enough to keep him quiet.’

‘Not it!’ cried Mr. Brambler jovially, as if he relished the prospect of a struggle, and would not willingly resign it. ‘It’ll just seem to poke him up a bit, an’ mek him burn the hotter. It’s beknown fur an’ wide what you taxed him with last night. I’m told he took all the Primitives to witness as he meant to persecute you.’

‘Yes,’ father said, ‘he undertook to prosecute.’

‘Prosecute or persecute, it’s all the same,’ said Mr. Brambler.

I don’t suppose that father had any idea of correcting the speech of so big a man, but if he had the big man was not willing to submit to the correction.

‘Niver you concern yourself with new-fangled modes o’ speech, Salter. The words as was good enough for my father is good enough for me. He threatened public to persecute you, did he?’

He asked the question for the sole purpose of getting the disputed word in and triumphing over it.

‘Yes,’ said father, humouring him, ‘he threatened to persecute.’

‘Public, I understand?’ said Mr. Brambler. ‘Afront of all the Primitives.’

‘Yes,’ said father, ‘the threat was public.’

‘Then he can’t go back, or if he did he’d have to fly the countryside. He’s got to go through with it, and he’s got me to tackle, Salter, an’ I’m bad to beat. I’ve been talkin’ to the inspector, an’ I’ve had a tip or two. He’ll apply at the police-court for a summons, an’ it’s liker than not, you’ll have a bobby walkin’ down here with a bit o’ paper. Send to me, or come to me, that minute, an’ I’ll put Lawyer Jackson on the job. It’s the deep pocket as wins in this here kind o’ game, an’ wheer Bill Sim can show a shillin’ I can show five pound—maybe ten. Mek your mind easy, Salter. I’ve gi’en my knife a little bit of a turn a’ready this afternoon, an’ the next time I get a chance, I’ll mek it a twister for him.’

So the good heathen departed, rejoicing that he had his enemy on the hip, and as it seemed, and seems to me, rejoicing not altogether unnaturally or wrongly, considering what manner of man the enemy had proved himself to be.

As it happened, Mr. Sim’s own case came off before a word was heard of his against father. The magistrates sat in petty sessions at Barfield on Saturdays and Wednesdays, and on the following Saturday Mr. Sim was fined twenty pounds, and ordered to pay costs. The very magistrates who made this order were called upon to grant a summons against father, and the same afternoon it was served upon him. He read the whole document aloud to mother and me, and its legal phraseology made a great impression upon us. I never see or hear the words 'Victoria, by the grace of God' without recalling that chilly night, the fog clinging to the window, the feeble flicker of the little, insufficient fire, and the gleam of the candlelight.

Father was cited to appear on the following Saturday.

I have never in my life since that time had anything to do with a criminal action for libel, and I have long since forgotten if I ever understood at that early age the technicalities involved. If there were any bail necessary, Mr. Brambler found it, I presume; but I remember no question of the sort.

But when the Saturday came, I, being pretty sure that I should not be allowed to see anything of the all-important affair of the day if I gave any sign of a desire to witness it, got up early, and, providing myself with a piece of bread, slipped away from the house, and made my way to Castle Barfield in the raw cold of the winter morning.

I knew the police-court, which was not more than a couple of hundred yards on our side of Mr. Brambler's house, and I had passed it often enough on petty session days to know the loafing crowd that filled the footpath and flowed out devious into the horse-road whilst the magistrates' sitting lasted.

After all these years, if I were artist enough to do it, I could draw that crowd. I remember figures and faces, details of dress, attitudes, tones of voices, loud oaths, whisperings—a thousand things which, if seen and heard now, would fade from my memory in a fortnight. There is no observation like that of a child, and my experience leads me to believe that, if we carried into manhood the faculty which was natural to us all in infancy, what is called genius would cease to be a wonder.

I tried to profit by my own physical insignificance, and to sneak into court under the elbow of a stalwart policeman, who mounted guard at the door; but he took me by the collar and lifted me, pretty much as terrier lifts a rat.

'Stand back, there.'

'Oh, if you please, sir,' I whined, 'let me in.'

'Why would I let you in?' asked the policeman.

I looked up at him as if he were a tower.

'Please, sir,' I said, 'I'm John Salter's little boy.'

'Oh!' said the good peeler. 'Y'are, are ye? Then in ye go.'

For John Salter's case was the *cause célèbre* of Barfield, and the whole parish was excited over it, and fuming about it, and betting on it.

I was wedged in a human mass, for there were no seats for the crowd, but all were gathered in a small open space, and the breath would have been fairly squeezed out of my small body if some kindly navvy had not wrenched me out of the press and set me on a projecting ornament in the corner of the wall, from which coign of vantage I could see and hear as well as anybody.

I had got up earlier than usual, and I had been hanging about in the cold for hours, and now, with the stifling closeness of the place, I began to feel very queer and heavy. If I had not been propped up by the crowd, I should certainly have fallen from my perch; as it was, I went uncomfortably to sleep, and had vivid spurts of wakefulness, which showed me the Bench, and the witnesses, and the prisoner in the case being heard, in a series of sharp pictures.

At last I fell into a profound slumber, from which I was awakened by hearing a stentorian voice roar out 'John Salter.'

CHAPTER XI

MY father's deep voice answered 'Here,' and I saw him standing bareheaded beside a table, between the crowd and the Bench at which the magistrates were seated.

'This way,' said a policeman, tapping him on the shoulder, and motioning him towards the dock.

My father was in the act of obeying this command, when up darted a little sharp sort of a man with a pointed nose and rufous hair, and very heavy red eyebrows.

'Sit down, Salter,' said this personage; and then, smartly turning on the magistrates, 'Your worships,' said he, 'I appear for the defendant in this case, and I shall protest against a defendant in a case of libel—a man of spotless reputation, though of humble social position—being placed in that dock from which you have just dismissed a petty thief to prison. I shall be able to show your worships in a very little while the nature of the case against my client, and you will see that I am justified in claiming him for the consideration of the court.'

With that he sat down again as smartly as he had risen.

Then a slow, bulky man, with huge whiskers, and a look of having been up all night, got up, and said that the case was a criminal case, and the libel a peculiarly atrocious libel, and that the dock was the proper place for the defendant.

Before the bulky man had fairly severed his coat-tails in act to sit down, our little rat of a man was up again, demanding to know what precedent his friend could find for so preposterous a proposal. The gentleman with the huge whiskers, being obviously unprovided with a precedent, did not produce one, and the Bench, who had probably never had a case of libel under their consideration before, were undecided.

The three gentlemen composing the tribunal laid their heads together and whispered, and their clerk, who sat below, stood on tiptoe and added his head to the group.

After a consultation which lasted two or three minutes, the clerk sat down and the gentleman who sat in the middle of the bench spoke:

'We do not think it necessary that at this stage of the proceedings the defendant should be placed in the dock.'

In default of a local gentry the Barfield bench was stocked at the time of which I write with self-made men, some of whom had risen from the lowest ranks. They did their duty according to their lights, and were a very honest, sterling set.

The decision was no sooner given than a voice said:

'First blood to we! Brayvo our side!' and I saw Mr. Joseph Brambler sitting at the end of the table. Mr. Sim's attorney had hitherto obscured him from my view, but he had slightly changed his position.

'Mr. Brambler,' said the spokesman of the justices, 'I should warn you as the court will brook no honseemly hinterruption.'

'All right, Ingram,' said Mr. Brambler confidentially; 'I'll be quiet.'

'You will find it to your profit,' said the chairman with ruffled dignity. He added after a deliberate pause, '*Mister* Brambler,' with a marked emphasis on the courtesy title.

Then the man with the whiskers rose and made a speech in which he told the Bench that his client was a man of spotless reputation.

The *habitués* of the court who had seen Mr. Sim fined for having false weights one week before laughed at this, and a man in a black gown called out:

'Silence in the court!'

Then Mr. Sim's attorney went on to expound his case. This man Salter had levelled a charge against his client, a charge which was a charge of the deepest character, a charge which was a charge, if that charge could be proved, which would render him liable to be charged with one of the most atrocious crimes that a man could be charged with. And so he lumbered on, and though of course I hated Mr. Sim, I had a sort of half pity for him in contrasting this dull and lumpy person with the man Mr. Brambler had chosen to speak up for father.

In a blunder-headed, rambling way he did get out the story pretty much as it happened, but he translated that splendid outburst of wrath of which my father had been guilty into so much mere vulgar abuse. In fine, he would call Mr. Sim, who would confirm his statement, and if the facts of the case were disputed by the other side, he would call a half-score of witnesses.

So Mr. Sim came into the box and was sworn and kissed the book. He looked like a man going to be hanged, and the white-hot excitement in which he quivered seemed to lend a sort of dignity and impressiveness to his face.

In the business of my later life as a journalist I have noticed that fact often. I have seen a commonplace wretch condemned to death listening to his sentence with an expression quite transformed and changed. This fat greed was facing his fate and knew it, and for the time being the knowledge purged his facial grossness all away, and made his look memorable.

On Sunday last he was at the chapel of the Primitive Christians in Clink Lane? Yes. And the defendant, John Salter, was there preaching? Yes. And the defendant made a violent attack upon him personally? Yes. And so on until the story was told, but without allusion to the weights.

But when the whiskered man was through with Mr. Sim, our man got up. I was interested in a little trick he had by which he seemed to stimulate the lifting of a cloak over his right shoulder. It is a common trick with barristers, and this smart little Birmingham solicitor meant to be a barrister some day, and had got into this habit beforehand, I suppose.

'All this happened on last Sunday week, I believe?'

'On last Sunday week.'

'When you were drunk?'

'Drunk? I was no more drunk than you be.'

'If you are impertinent, witness, I shall have to ask for the protection of the Bench. Answer my question, if you please: Were you drunk or sober?'

'Sober.'

'Indeed! How many glasses of whisky can you hold?'

'I'm no whisky drinker.'

'You were at the Guest Arms on Sunday night, I think?' This with his keen head on one side, and his keen eye cocked at the witness.

Mr. Brambler was rubbing his hands with a keen enjoyment, and chuckling softly to himself.

'I looked in,' said Mr. Sim.

'You looked in for an hour, I think? Try to remember.'

'Nothin' like it.'

'Nothing like it? Very good. You drank eight glasses of Scotch whisky in something like an hour—eh?'

'I had a glass or two.'

'Very well. I shall call the landlord, who will swear that between half-past six and half-past seven you drank and paid for eight glasses of hot Scotch whisky. Shall you deny that?'

'I didn't count 'em.'

'Come, now, were you so tipsy as not to know what you paid?'

'I was sober as I am this minute.'

'Is that saying much?' said the smart solicitor.

Mr. Brambler threw himself back with a shout of triumphant laughter, and everybody laughed, except the officials and the witness. It was quite unfair, but the query helped to put Mr. Sim out of countenance, and that, of course, was what the smart solicitor wanted. But the chairman of the justices, with his old-fashioned Staffordshire notions of fair play, broke in:

'I see no sign o' drink about the witness. Pursue your cross-examination, sir.'

The little rat of a man bowed to the discernment of the Bench.

'We take it you were sober?'

'I was sober.'

'Then you remember what you paid when you left the Guest Arms? You are sober now, at all events, and you can tell me how much is eight times fourpence? Come, now, make an intellectual effort. Eight times fourpence?'

'Two an' eightpence.'

'Capital. Two and eightpence. And one half-crown and two penny-pieces will make two and eightpence?'

'I suppose so.'

'You suppose so? Don't juggle with the court, sir. On your oath, sir, do you know that simple fact, or do you not?'

'Course I do. Any kid knows that.'

'Of course you do, and of course any child does. Then why, sir, did you dare to prevaricate with the court?'

Mr. Sim looked helpless and all abroad.

'Now, sir, did you, or did you not, when you left the Guest Arms on Sunday last, pay for liquor consumed on the occasion of that visit the sum of two shillings and eightpence in the form of one half-crown and two penny-pieces? I shall ask you to remember that you are on your oath, sir, and that I am not questioning in the dark.'

'Well, I did,' said Mr. Sim; 'but they'm uncommon small four-pennorths at the Guest, an' I've said as much to Lisha Troman's face more than once.'

'And yet you are no whisky drinker!' said the sharp solicitor. 'Not being a whisky drinker, why do you take eight glasses in an hour and feel so keen an interest in the size of a four-pennorth? Very well, Mr. Sim; of course you don't have to answer that question. But having consumed eight glasses of whisky in very much less than an hour, and being quite sober, you set out to walk to the Primitive Christians' Chapel in Clink Lane. Just so. And being a shade too sober for your own fancy, you made a call at the Museum Tavern? How many Scotch whiskys there?'

'One,' said Mr. Sim.

'And how many at the Fox and Dogs?'

'One,' said Mr. Sim.

'And how many at the Grapes?'

'One,' said Mr. Sim.

'And where did you make up the dozen?'

'Nowhere.'

'Very well. Now, having consumed eleven glasses of whisky in an hour or thereabouts, and being perfectly sober, you felt yourself in a mood for Christian worship? Eh? Tell us that, if you please.'

'I turned in to sit down a bit.'

‘You didn’t go in with the express purpose of making a disturbance, did you?’

‘No; I didn’t.’

‘If the Bench thinks it worth while that I continue this examination——?’ said the sharp solicitor. ‘It is within the knowledge of the Bench that the complainant was fined in this court for keeping false weights only this day week, and I have extracted from him the fact that he was shamefully intoxicated on the night now in question.’

‘We admit this hevidence,’ said the chairman, with great dignity, ‘but the charge has not yet been touched upon. The Bench is advised as justification or disproof is the only defence. Pursoo your case, sir. You ’ave the the attention of the court.’

Again the little man bowed to the will of the court. If he had known as much of the court’s temper as even I could have told him, he would have been a shade less soapy with it. There was nothing your old-fashioned mid-Englander hated like soft-sawder. That was a red rag to the bull at any minute of the day.

‘Now, being perfectly sober after eleven glasses of hot Scotch whisky, you went to chapel, Mr. Sim. Did you interrupt the service?’

Mr. Sim made a mighty effort and pulled himself together.

‘Might I tell this my own way?’ he asked. ‘This chap mythers me.’

‘Very well, sir,’ said the solicitor; ‘tell it in your own way, but remember that I have the right to question you. Now go on.’

‘I’d no sooner got into the pläace,’ said Mr. Sim, ‘an’ sat down quiet to rest mysen, than this Jack Salter sets about me an’ charges me wi’ all manner o’ crimes.’

‘Wait a bit. What kind of crimes?’

‘Why, he charged me wi’ gettin’ men together an’ payin’ ’em to half-kill him an’ Parson Allardyce.’

‘Yes, yes. But wait a bit. Did he charge you with keeping false weights? Come now, when you had brutally interrupted the service, did he denounce you as a man who notoriously kept three sets of weights? Tell the court that, if you please, Now, did he?’

‘Yis,’ said Mr. Sim, ‘he did, blast him!’

At this the whole court roared, Bench and all, and Mr. Sim glared round with a baffled exasperation so complete that we laughed for a full minute.

'If I'd got you and him outside,' said the badgered rascal, amidst a new outburst of laughter, 'you'd smile on t'other side.'

'Well now, Mr. Sim, we will get on with the case. You are, of course, a man of amiable temper?'

'I'm as hamiable as any one heer,' said Mr. Sim, 'when I'm let alone.'

'And you are quite sure that you made no disturbance in chapel?'

'Not until he began to knock my good näam about.'

'Your good name? As a notorious dealer in false weights?'

'You can get past that, sir,' said the chairman of the Bench. 'That's no part o' the libel charged agen your client.'

'Quite so, your worship. I may as well say at once that we plead justification for that part of the libel which is charged against us just as openly as we do for that part which is so judiciously suppressed by Mr. Sim. Now, Mr. Sim, attend to me.'

'Goo it, lawyer!' said Mr. Brambler, in such a state of excitement that he could not contain himself. 'Tackle him!'

'Mr. Brambler,' said the chairman, 'if the court is again broke in upon i' this wise, the Bench'll be compelled to tek notice on it.'

'I beg the Bench's pardon, Ingram,' said Mr. Brambler. 'It slipt out unawares like.'

'Don't let it slip out again,' said the chairman. 'Now, sir, pursoo your interrogations.'

'You allege, Mr. Sim,' said the solicitor, settling his visionary barrister's robe upon his shoulder, 'that the defendant charged you in public with having bribed a number of men to assault him.'

'It's fause!' cried Sim. 'I bribed nobody.'

'That is the point we want to arrive at. Do you happen to know a man named Aminadab Ault?'

'There is such a man.'

'There is such a man. Do you know him?'

'I know him to look at.'

'Do you know him to speak to?'

'The man's dealt wi' me this five-an'-twenty 'ear.'

'And there is such a man, and you know him to look at. Very well.' (Barrister's gown again.) 'Do you know Job Rusker?'

'Yes.'

'Do you know him to look at?'

'He's dealt wi' me a long time.'

'Do you know Edward Tunley?'

Mr. Sim began to mop his forehead with his sleeve.

'Do you know Edward Tunley?'

'Yis, yis; I know the man. Why shouldn't I know him? You'm talkin' about folks as I was born an' bred among.'

'Do you know Abraham Hotchkiss?'

'Worked for me for years,' said Mr. Sim.

'And do you know Abel Dodge?'

'No. Niver heerd o' the man.'

'Goes by the name o' Blowhard,' said father across the table.

'Oho! Do you know a man who goes by the name of Blowhard?'

'Yis, I know him well enough.'

'Now, is it a fact that all these men are deep in your debt?'

'No,' cried Sim; 'theer isn't one o' 'em as owes me a farthin'.'

For a moment the solicitor looked non-plussed, but my father said quietly, 'Ask him since when,' and he recovered himself at once.

'When did they get out of debt?'

'Months ago.'

'Two months ago?'

'More nor that.'

'And all at the same time?'

'No. Different times.'

'How far apart? Come, now. You keep books. I shall ask to see them. When did these men get out of your debt? Come now. You've a very good memory, Mr. Sim. You can tell us what you paid for drink last Sunday. Try to remember this. This, your worships, is a most important point, and I shall ask for an order for the production of the witness's books.'

'They'll tell you nothin',' said the witness, smearing his low forehead with his palm. The sweat was standing there in beads before his hand had fallen to his side.

'Perhaps you will tell us something. Now, on your oath, how much did these men owe you? There were five of them, and they all worked for you, and they were in your debt. For how much? Don't be particular to a shilling.'

‘They might have owed a five-pound note among ’em.’

‘And they all cleared themselves?’

‘Yis, they did.’

‘Within a week of each other. Wasn’t that curious?’

Mr. Sim was in a condition to drop into any trap that might be set for him, but the Bench intervened.

‘You put words into the witness’s mouth. He hasn’t said they paid within a week. Fair play’s a jewel.’

‘With all submission to the Bench, I thought the witness had admitted that. In any case, your worships, it is understood that they all paid, and all paid within a very short time. Now, didn’t that strike you as curious, Mr. Sim?’

‘They payin’ when they can?’

‘Exactly. But how did they come to pay all at one time, or nearly at one time?’

‘How should I know?’

‘You didn’t wipe off their debts, did you?’

‘Wipe off their debts? What should I wipe off their debts for?’

‘Why, indeed? But did you? Come, Mr. Sim, it was you who challenged this case. We may be a little stronger than you think. Did you wipe off the debts of these men, or any portion of them?’

‘Well,’ said Mr. Sim, ‘I’ve allays made a p’int of dealin’ merciful with old customers.’

‘You have never given them too much weight to carry, for example?’

At this uprose Mr. Brambler, and slapped the solicitor on the back. I can only think he had been drinking.

‘By gosh, lad!’ he said, ‘they told me you was worth your money. Mek it double if you like. You’m welcome!’

The solicitor looked less pleased at this public expression of approval than Mr. Brambler had evidently expected. He fell back beneath the sharp man’s eye, and met the disapproval of the Bench with a crush and discomfited air.

‘I won’t offend again, Ingram,’ he said humbly, ‘I’ll niver offend again.’

‘The court’ll feel compelled to deal wi’ you, Mr. Brambler,’ said the speaking magistrate (the other two were dumb from start to finish, except for whispers across and across to each other), 'when this case has come to a close.'

'So be it,' said Mr. Brambler submissively, and the case went on again.

'Very well, then,' pursued the solicitor, with a vengeful sideway look on Mr. Brambler and a dignified hitch at the visionary gown. 'You were merciful to these poor fellows, and you forgave them what they owed you. And what other inducement did you offer them to assault the defendant? '

'I niver axed 'em to assault the defendant.'

'Now, be very careful. You are not bound to answer any question which may criminate yourself, and you need not answer unless you please. But if you answer untruly, it is my duty to tell you that you stand open to one of the gravest charges known to the law. What inducement did you offer these men to assault the defendant and the Reverend Mr. Allardyce? '

'I niver had any spite agen Mr. Allardyce.'

'Very well. But answer my question. What inducement did you offer these men for the deed which I shall prove they committed at your instigation? You are not compelled to answer. But remember. you are on your oath.'

The witness once more smeared his palm across his forehead, and looked around like a baited bull, but he returned no word of reply.

'It does not appear to me to be worth while to pursue this cross-examination further, your worships,' said the solicitor. 'We are in a position to prove that the men whom I have named practically confessed the crime, and that they were forgiven in a spirit of Christian charity, which few of us can emulate, by the men they had brutally assaulted—the Reverend Mr. Allardyce and my client. The witness, under pressure, does not seem inclined to swear that he did not commit the terrible and atrocious crime attributed to him. The consequences of that crime have been endured by my client in two months of bitter suffering. All that he has forgiven; but, in a moment of natural and righteous anger, he has denounced this amiable gentleman, who, having first hired a set of scoundrels to assault him, now proposes to send him to prison for having complained. I throw myself unreservedly upon the court.'

The little man put his heart into it, and when he sat down the room rang with a shout, against which the man in the stuff cloak shouted ' Order in court! ' in vain.

The Bench consulted.

'We find that theer is no case agen the defendant,' said their spokeman, ' an' the charge is dismissed accordin'.'

There was another burst of cheering, led by Mr. Joseph Brambler, who had mounted on his seat and waved his hat in his enthusiasm.

This hot fit was not cooled when Mr. Brambler—silence being restored—was ordered to stand up.

' Mr. Brambler,' said the chairman, ' I shall do my dooty. I am well aweer as you are one of the most respected citizens o' this parish, an' the pain o' the court is theerfore all the deeper as it should be compelled to deal with you; but you have broke the order of the court repeated, and it is felt by the Bench to be their dooty to fine you forty shillin's.'

Mr. Brambler, smiling and rosy, thrust his hand into his pocket and pulled out a heap of money, from which he selected two sovereigns ; he handed these to the clerk at the table, and turned jovially to the Bench.

'There you be, Ingram, and theer's my forty shillin's. Come and dine wi' me tomorrow, all three on ye, an' I'll give you as good a feed as iver you sat outside on in your lives.'

And then downstairs and out of doors streamed everybody, with roaring cheers. Mr. Joseph waving his hat until it was a wonder it did not part from the brim, and shouting until he was hoarse.

Mr. Sim, for prudential reasons, stayed inside, and when his face appeared at a corridor window, such a spontaneous yell of execration arose that he drew back again and hid himself.

I heard afterwards that he had to secure a carriage and drive away in the afternoon darkness from the court, taking a circuitous road which added half a dozen miles to his journey home.

' Hillo, young whipper-snapper! ' cried Mr. Brambler, discerning me in the crowd; ' beest thee here? Theer's half a crown for ye. This day's cost me a bit o' money, Salter,' he added to my father; ' but I'm main contented.'

He looked as if he were, at least; but father was very quiet about his triumph.

'You're a moderate man, I know, Salter,' said Mr. Brambler; 'but on the top o' this you shall have a glass o' beer, if you niver taste another.'

He bundled us off—father, and the solicitor who had so cleverly defended him, and me—to his own house, and he made father sit down in the wonderful palatial parlour, and there he compelled him to drink a glass of sherry (the first and last wine he ever tasted except in his sickness), and he paid the solicitor in our presence in ready money.

'An', my gosh!' he said admiringly, 'how you did turn that chap inside out.'

I can't guess what premonition was in my father's mind, but he was very quiet and subdued.

'This is a day,' cried Mr. Brambler, 'as some on us'll remember for many a 'ear to come.'

'Some on us may,' said father; 'but this business isn't over yet.'

They asked him what he meant and what he afeard.

'I'm none afear'd,' he said, with a sort of tranquil sadness; 'but that's how I feel about it. It isn't over yet.'

They laughed at him, but they did not seem to change his humour, and as he led me home, holding my hand all the way as he had used to do when I was very much younger and smaller, I felt as if a shadow were upon me.

CHAPTER XII

I CAN honestly say that during the two months of life that were left to him my father worked like an apostle. With Mr. Brambler now behind him as his fast and devoted friend, he set foot on a number of enterprises which would otherwise have been impossible for him. Among them were a Sunday afternoon ragged-school and a night-school for boys. He spent his days in the attempt to consolidate a feeble and tottering institution which had never had any real vitality in it—the Nailers' Union.

He tried to establish a co-operative provision shop for the men, and he could have done it with Mr. Brambler's aid, but the plain truth is that the nailers themselves would have nothing to say to him. Out of the ranks of his own class I have never known a man more universally respected, but within those ranks he was hated.

He was anathema marantha to the little dealers, and that was only natural, because he was spending all his days in fighting against their oppressions and extortions. But the men hated him because to be seen in his company, even to be visited by him, was to bring down the wrath of the oppressor. The poor wretches were so hopelessly down that they had abandoned all hope of ever being up again, and they were under a bondage so cruelly severe, that any sensible tightening of the chain meant misery absolute and complete in place of the scarce qualified misery in which they passed their lives already.

'These chaps are slaves,' he told Mr. Allardyce once in my hearing, 'and slaves they will be so long as they live. The only chance o' doin' anythin' with 'em is to catch the young uns, an' teach them summat of independence.'

But in spite of this conclusion, which I know was rooted in his mind, he could not leave the men themselves alone; and though he was patient with them as a rule, he did not spare hard words at times. He got badly handled at Quarrymoor one night for telling a crowd of them that their cowardice was answerable for the miserable condition, and he lived in an atmosphere of threats and insult.

'I speak as one o' yorselves,' he said on another night to a little company he had gathered from amongst our neighbours in our own house.

'One o' we?' a listener retorted. 'Why, when didst thee lay hand to homber last?'

The whole enterprise was heart-breaking and impossible, in fact, and as his efforts increased so opposition grew.

Mr. Brambler had found a cottage room for a night-school, and father had secured half a dozen pupils. He might perhaps have had more if he could have afforded it, but his method of attracting them was by paying the parents of each child sixpence a week as an offset against loss of time.

Three of these waifs had by some miracle learned their letters and their *a b, ab,* and could read simple words. Three of them were quite unlettered, and at my father's order I took the lower class in hand, and for a few weeks—until, indeed, the end came—I instructed it in the mysteries of the alphabet.

My pupils were all very much bigger and older than myself, and I had a sore time of it all. The biggest boy of all was one Jack Randall, and on one occasion I had a personal encounter with him which was much to my disadvantage. I had provided for me a board on which was pasted a sheet of paper, and on the paper the alphabet was printed irregularly. *A* was somewhere near the middle and *Z* was near the beginning.

'What's that?' said I, setting the point of a short stick on the letter *A*. Nobody answered, but all three stared at it as if it were something foreign. They had been through a straightforward alphabet every night for a week past, but this innovation puzzled them.

'That's *A*,' said I, when I thought I had waited long enough.

'You're a liar!' said Jack Randall; 'that's no more *A* than I be.'

'That's *A*,' I insisted, strong in knowledge.

'How do you know?'

'Why, becos it is.'

'Look here,' said Jack Randall, 'if thee talkest to me like that I'll poonch thy yed.'

He made up his mind so suddenly to put this project into instant execution that I was on my back before I knew it.

Master Randall was banished for the rest of the evening, but I scarcely dared to insist on my own knowledge afterwards.

Mr. Allardyce of course looked in on us sometimes, and on occasion, we had a visit from Mr. Joseph Brambler. Then Mr. Jeremiah began to take an interest in us, and learning that my father's chief trouble was want of pupils and that pupils were to be had by purchase, he went out and bought a dozen, and conveyed them into the room in triumph. They crowded us in conveniently, and were really in so very small a space too many for our hands; but they eased us of this difficulty by playing truant in a body next night. Mr. Jeremiah was extremely well-meaning in the matter, and on his next visit hunted up a few of them, and these at his cost became pretty regular pupils.

We used to think Mr. Jeremiah a little mad, and perhaps he was, but we all got to like him. He made quite a hobby of the little night-school, and once when father was compelled to be absent, because of a labour meeting in the district at which he had to speak, Mr. Jeremiah took his place. There was not a great deal of study that evening, but at least we were entertained. We had a black-board and a piece of chalk for the simple studies in arithmetic of which our most advanced boys were capable, and I think I can see Mr. Jeremiah now, as he dusted that board with a silk handkerchief, and, arranging the two candles on either side of it, took the piece of chalk in his fingers, and surveyed his small audience of eight or nine.

'I'll do you a bit of art work, lads,' he said, his face beaming with that almost childish self-complacency I had seen in him so often. 'I used to be a Don at that. What should you like to see, now? Should you like to see a beautiful lady? '

We were all eager to see a beautiful lady, and Mr. Jeremiah, with a good deal of posturing beforehand, and a great waving of his chalk in the air, began to draw. If my memory is at all trustworthy, he drew very cleverly. We could not make out at first what he was trying for, but in a little while, in white against the black, there was a very pretty head, with ringlets on either side the face.

'I was a real Don at this once on a time, lads,' said Mr. Jeremiah when the hand-clapping and the 'Oh's!' were all silent. 'Would you like to see a nigger, now? or a Chinyman? or the divil?'

Some cried for one, and some for another, but one lad sang out for all three.

'Very well,' said the amiable creature, 'you shall have all three.'

It was delightful to see him at work, he put such boyish gusto into it, and boasted and swaggered with such relish. We all shouted and clapped hands for the nigger and the Chinaman, and the devil created a perfect furore. He was as happy as a child till then, but on one calling out to him for something else, he grew moody on a sudden, and dusted out the devil with a face of melancholy.

'It's all wrong somehow,' he said mournfully; 'I used to think I was a Don at it, but I niver shall be. I tried the drapery trade when I was a lad, and I made no hand o' that. Then I was apprenticed to the music for five or six years. I studied under the best local professors, but I never made a Don at it. Then I went in for the paintin' and studied that, but I niver made a Don at it. I was in Belgium for three 'ears a-studyin' in Antwerp.' He paused sadly, and wiped his eyes with the handkerchief he had used to dust the blackboard. I don't know how the other lads felt, but I was conscious of a sense of unmerited defeat somewhere, and was very sorry for him, though I knew the feeling to be presumptious and impertinent. 'I was three years in Antwerp,' he said, brightening suddenly, 'an' I learned to speak French theer.' He saddened as suddenly as he had brightened. 'I niver made a Don at it. I'm fifty-eight, I am, an' I'm beginnin' to think I shall never mek a Don at anythin'.'

'Oh, Mr. Jeremiah,' I was constrained to say, 'your music's beautiful!'

'Ah!' he said and smiled, 'you've heerd me play.'

He made a motion which I understood as if he had a 'cello in his hands, and were drawing the bow across the strings. The action was unmeaning and grotesque to a handful of lads who had never seen the instrument, and there was a smothered laugh at it. The rapt look faded off his face, and the corners of his mouth went down.

'You can go home, lads,' he said; and taking up his hat, he

walked solemnly out of the house, leaving us all, I think, rather uncomfortable for the moment.

He came again, next night, however, in as good a humour as we had ever seen him in, and sat beaming amongst us while we went through our routine lessons. When these were over the lads clamoured for Mr. Jeremiah to draw again, but he would not be persuaded.

'No, my b'ys,' he said gravely, 'that's a waste o' time. I've got summat better than that. I come by Chance the grocer's, in Barfield High Street, to-night. Do you know what he's got in his winder?'

One boy guessed cheese, and another sugar, but Mr. Jeremiah shook his head.

'Better than them,' he said 'He's got a great big bowl full of bran'-new penny-pieces. I went in an' bought a dozen on 'em. Look at 'em.'

They glistened like gold as he turned them over in his extended palm.

'Now, Salter, who's the best scholard here?'

Father named his most docile and obedient pupil.

'Then here's a bran'-new penny-piece for him,' said Mr. Jeremiah. 'An' who's the next best? This little feller? Then here's a bran'-new penny-piece for him. An' who's the next best?'

All the students got a penny each, and made as much of it as if it were a sovereign.

'An' now, my b'ys,' said Mr. Jeremiah, 'I shall do that for ivery lad as comes here ivery night till Christmas—that is, for them as is well reported on by the gaffer.'

We gave Mr. Jeremiah three hearty cheers.

It is strange to think that the intrusion of this unharmful creature into our affairs should have orphaned me and left my mother a widow and yet it happened so.

I have never blamed poor Mr. Jeremiah, for, in any case, the storm would have broken upon us, and there were signs enough that it was brewing.

We were setting ourselves up to be better than our neighbours; we were making enmities between those neighbours and the foggers by whose good will they lived. My father had taken to wearing a shirt collar; that's a curious thing to put in a fatal indictment—a count of life and death—and yet they put it there. My father's ill-spared bribe to each of his scholars, and Mr. Jeremiah's pence, brought pupils still, but they came in defiance of their fathers and mothers, because they came against the countenance of the foggers; and the night-school bred dissension in many households. Angry men came and took away their sons, often enough with violence, and always with threats of violence.

Latterly it came to pass that there was a nightly scene, and the roughs of the district—who were plentiful, Heaven knows!—hung about in anticipation of it, and enjoyed it hugely when it came.

I look back, and I think of it all with wonder, and yet with understanding. Here was a man who was spending his life in unremitting labour for the good of those about him—a man who, born in any other place in life, would have made for himself a name; a man of heart and brains; a man of courage, pity and endurance—and every worthy faculty he had made him hateful to those for whom he laboured. He would have buttered their scanty bread for them, and have made it plentiful, if they would have allowed him to do it; but they thought he would rob them of what they had, and so, quite naturally, they hated him.

They had no courage to rise out of the slough they lay in, and they were angry with him because he had dared to do the thing which frightened them in the mere contemplation. Fierce, and ignorant, and hungry, bold in the mass, and cowardly when taken singly, they were no more civilized in a single generation than a pack of wolves.

God forbid that I should even seem to lump them all in one basket, for my father came of their stock, and many another good man, too, as I can well believe; but I speak of them in the mass, and I know that they were what the generations had made them.

On that last night Mr. Allardyce was with us. I wish he had been anywhere else in the world, for he was not the sort of man one parts with lightly, or whose place in the world is soon filled. He came in smiling and cheerful, and shook hands with father and mother and patted me on the head.

'And how's the night-school, Salter? I've come down to have another look at it, for I'm going into Hampshire to-morrow, to take the work of a friend of mine, and I may not be back for a month or more.'

'They're fallin' away, sir,' said father, with a kind of settled sadness. 'I've one lad left, and only one. They tek me fo. theii enemy, poor things, an' they're all against our plans.'

'Never mind; courage and trust, Salter—courage and trust.'

'Ay, sir,' said father; 'the sum'll work out all right in the end, no doubt. But we're the only figures in it; and, for my own part, sir, I feel as if I stood for nought without a figure before me.'

'We're all down-hearted at times,' said Mr. Allardyce, lightly enough for him, who was commonly so serious. 'Shall we go?'

They went, and went to a grim ending, and I went with them, not because I was of any use to father's one big pupil, but because it had come to be a habit, and I did my own lessons at the night-school.

The road was pretty well alive in front of the cottage where Mr. Brambler had hired the room for us, and Mr. Allardyce was hustled, as well as father. It was done by apparent accident, but nobody was deceived by that. One fellow, a collier, if one might judge by the flannel clothes he wore, lurched heavily against the curate and staggered him. The man must have been there for the mere sport of the thing, for the colliers, at any rate, had no grudge against us.

'Have a little care, my friend,' said Mr. Allardyce quite mildly, and somebody from behind knocked his silk hat clean over his eyes.

He freed himself from it and looked round, but the night was dark, and the nearest street lamp was forty yards away, so that he could make out nobody with any clearness.

'Will the man who did that show himself?' he asked. 'It isn't a very plucky thing to hit a man from behind, is it, boys?'

The only response was a 'boo-boo!' of many voices from the outside edge of the crowd, and a rush which swayed the people who stood nearest against us.

'Better come in, sir,' said father. 'They'll be bent on mischief if we stop here.'

At the instant at which we entered the room and closed the door a brick was thrown, and broke into fragments on the wall of the house.

'What does all this mean, Salter?' asked Mr. Allardyce. 'They cheered you in Barfield High Street only two months ago.'

'Not the nailers,' said father. 'There's plenty here only for sport to-night, but there's plenty more for mischief, and I wish you were safe at home, Mr. Allardyce.'

'My dear Salter,' cried the curate, 'there's nothing to be afraid of. But you have no pupils here yet. I'm afraid that with this crowd outside there's little chance of school to-night.'

'Little chance, indeed, sir,' said father; and as he spoke the door opened.

'Here's your pupil,' said Mr. Allardyce, and in came Mr. Jeremiah, holding father's one pupil by the ear.

'This is a pretty sort of rumpus, this is, Salter,' said he. 'I picked up this chap outside. I've paid him to come for his schoolin' an' now to-night he says he'll see me damned fust. So I just fetched him along, an' here he is.'

'There can be no school to-night,' said Mr. Allardyce, 'with this noise going on about us. I am afraid, Salter, that we shall have to abandon the scheme for a time. It will be more politic, perhaps. We can withdraw a little, to leap the better later on.'

'You're not afeard o' this riff-raff, are you?' asked Mr. Jeremiah. 'I'll let 'em know who's who!'

There was a rising storm of hoots and groans outside, and now and again a missile, hurled at hazard struck the door. I could scarcely hear what was said.

'Better let em quiet down,' said father.

'Leave 'em to me,' said Mr. Jeremiah. He walked to the door and opened it. 'Do you fellers know who I am?' he asked.

Somebody on the edge of the crowd bawled 'Mad Jerry!' and there was a great shout of laughter.

'Let me get at that feller!' he cried, and as he moved forward something struck him on the shoulder. At this he hit out at the man nearest to him, and in as little time as it takes to tell it he was down. At the same second of time a stone crashed through the window, and knocked over the solitary candle on the table. I saw all the rest dimly in the darkness, but father and Mr. Allardyce charged out to rescue their companion, and in an instant, as it seemed, the whole mob was upon them. There was a mad welter and confusion, a shifting mass of figures, and nothing seen distinctly; but I heard the noise of blows, and a roar of oaths and curses, and I stood there shuddering and helpless in the darkness.

How long the *mêlée* lasted I cannot even guess. The fight was not all on one side, for I heard loud cries for fair play, and the thing lasted much too long to have been a mere struggle of two against three hundred. But shivering and crying bitterly in the darkness there, I heard that the confused noise grew fainter, and I saw the struggling figures fewer and fewer. The crowd seemed to break up and melt, and I heard a clattering of thick-booted feet upon the frozen wintry road. Then there came a dreadful silence, and I thought at first that the mob had carried father and Mr. Allardyce away to work some mischief on them, for there was not a soul left in sight. But venturing from the door, I heard the crowd retreating in three directions—along the road on either side and down the lane in front.

I was frightened, as I had reason to be, and I called out for father as loudly as my shaking sobs would let me. Not a sound came in answer, and running blindly forward, I fell upon a prostage figure. I explored it with my hands in a passion of terror.

'I didn't mek a Don at that job, nayther,' groaned poor Jerry Brambler.

He never spoke again.

I stood shrieking there, and not a living creature came near me. I tore my throat with cries. I besought Mr. Jeremiah to tell me where father was, but he gave no sign.

The night was dark as pitch, for some chance missile had smashed the glass of the only lamp in the street, and the wind had taken the light away from the burner.

I knelt on the icy ground and held for comfort to Mr. Jeremiah's hand. It was warm when I first took it, and it seemed to give me a sort of courage, but it grew colder and colder and colder and colder, and at last it was so cold it frightened me.

I do not know who found me, or at what hour I was found, but I know that I awoke in the old home room, and that on the bed lay a figure outlined under a rough sheet. That was all that was left of my father, who amongst his own class is remembered to this day in Quarrymoor and Castle Barfield as a man who deserted his class for gain.

THE BLACK COUNTRY SOCIETY OFFER A WIDE VARIETY OF PUBLICATIONS AND OTHER MATERIAL OF LOCAL INTEREST AT ATTRACTIVE PRICES.

THEY INCLUDE

Any or all backnumbers of the Blackcountryman quarterly magazine.

PVC binders to hold twelve copies.

Black Country Humour (local jokes and anecdotes)

Bostin Fittle (recipes and hints)

Powered Vehicles made in the Black Country (New enlarged edition)

Jim and Kate (dialect poems)

Boulton and Watt and the Soho Undertakings.

The Limestone Mines of Walsall (historical study).

For full list and prices write to Mrs. P. M. Purcell,
15 Clayton Road, Wall Heath, Kingswinford
West Midlands DY6 0HR

Also available:
Maps – Medallions – Commemorative Postal Covers.

ALWAYS SOMETHING NEW IN THE PIPELINE